REBEL PRINCE

For Malcolm MacIldowie, chief of the Clan Glenallan, it began on an ordinary spring evening in London, while he was whiling away the time at the gambling rooms of the courtly set. For it was then that the word was passed to him in a whisper, "Bonnie Prince Charlie has sailed!"

That was the signal for which that young Scottish hothead had waited his youthful lifetime. He wasted no time in returning to his beloved mountains, in rallying his loyal clansmen, and setting out. Through the hills they marched, rousing the Camerons and the MacDonalds, alerting the Grants, the MacPhersons, the Robertsons.

And when Charles Edward Stuart, the Young Pretender, set foot at last on Scotland's soil, he found Glenallan and eight hundred determined warriors waiting for him to lead them through blood and fire to the British throne—or to death!

DONALD BARR CHIDSEY needs little introduction to readers of historical novels for his many excellent books have gained him a reputation for both historical accuracy and thrilling adventure. His previous Ace books include THIS BRIGHT SWORD (D-278) and CAPTAIN CROSSBONES (D-318). Author also of many factual biographies, including one of Bonnie Prince Charlie, he says of THE PIPES ARE CALLING:

"The principal characters, the hero, heroine, and villain, are fictional, but many of the others, in fact most of them, were real persons. Lord Barrymore, Donald of Lochiel, Mr. Secretary Murray, the Young Clanranald, Cluny MacPherson and the Young MacPherson, Patrick Grant and the Seven Men of Glenmoriston, even Evan MacGregor, the first Highlander into Edinburgh, actually existed."

The Pipes Are Calling

by

DONALD BARR CHIDSEY

ACE BOOKS, INC.
23 West 47th Street, New York 36, N. Y.

CHAPTER 1

IT LACKED AN HOUR OF midnight when Lord Barrymore entered Martin's, in Hockley-in-the-Hole, but already the tables were crowded. Around three sides of the Long Room gentlemen sat playing whist-and-honors—quiet, most of them, very serious. There were three large hazard tables in the center of the room, all crowded. Other gentlemen, gathered at steaming punch bowls, were merely engaged in getting drunk.

Lord Barrymore walked in and out of the crowds, smiling to left and right, and nodding to acquaintances as they smiled and nodded to him. He refused many invitations to stop and play, or stop and drink. He had more important things to think about.

At last he saw the man he wanted—a tall young Scot dressed in brown broadcloth and narrow Irish lace. Here was a glum fellow; and glumness was not the rule at Martin's. His luck was bad: he had just thrown aces and on the next roll had crabbed. But that was not the reason for his dourness; he was by nature somber, and it was clear from his manner that he took little delight in his surroundings and had little love for his fellow gamesters.

"Seven," he called, and began to cast again. Six, five, nine, ten fell out. On the other side of the table Captain Fitzstephen had been winning. The others busied themselves making side bets.

Aces fell—four, nine. It was a long roll.

Lord Barrymore took a place at the table next to the caster. His manner was that of a gentleman who would watch for his own amusement, perhaps side-betting a little, but not gaming in earnest. Nevertheless, he spoke to the Scot in a low voice.

5

"You are the Young Glenallan?"

"Aye."

Malcolm of Glenallan glanced up, nodded, then returned to his casting.

"D'ye remember me?"

"Aye. You are my Lord Barrymore."

The newcomer drew a snuffbox from a waistcoat pocket, took a sniff, snapped the box shut. He was nervous about this business. He wanted to keep the other players under the impression that he had come merely to pass the time and that the caster was the most casual of his acquaintances.

"Heed me carefully, Glenallan, and don't show any emotion at what I tell you. Prince Charles is coming."

Four, five, eleven, then a six. Would this roll go on forever? The caster's expression did not change; he pretended not even to hear, but inwardly he was so agitated that he forgot to pick up his winnings, or even to notice that he *had* won; and Captain Fitzstephen, assuming that this meant a doubled bet, threw twenty pounds on the table. Elsewhere the currency clinked as those who had bet with the dice collected their winnings.

"Six!"

The dice fell four and two. He left the money on the table, and Fitzstephen, no longer grinning, covered it with forty pounds.

"Seven!"

He nicked with eleven, left the money on the table, picked up the dice again.

Meanwhile, Lord Barrymore was talking. Occasionally raising his voice, he commented upon the caster's sudden good luck or congratulated a fortunate side better. But for the most part his voice, very low, was heard only by the man for whom it was intended.

"You are to depart for your home immediately. They will

tell you there where to go. The landing will be somewhere near your estate. The Cameron of Fassden will inform you."

Malcolm of Glenallan called eight and threw six, called seven and threw eleven. He never touched the money, which increased rapidly. There were murmurs of amazement at his luck and daring, for he had previously seemed a cautious gambler. The truth was, he was casting in a daze, and did not realize how much he was winning, or how much he was risking.

Captain Fitzstephen, his face a thundercloud, drank heavily from a punch glass that had been brought to him, and continued to cover the bet on the table.

"Has he sailed already?"

Malcolm's heart was pounding furiously. The room and all its bright colors were a monstrous blur to him.

"Sh-sh! Don't even speak the name. Yes, he has sailed. But until he lands we must be careful as cats, Glenallan. No mention of this to— Lord, man, you're not quitting when the luck's running with you?" he cried aloud.

For Glenallan had started to pick up the money and had pushed the dice away, though it was still his cast. There was only one thought on his mind now. He wanted to be going north to join his father and his clansmen. Gambling was forgotten. Charlie had sailed . . .

"Quitting, Jocky?"

It was plain that Fitzstephen was dangerously angry. He had lost all his winnings and no little part of his own money as well, on this one long remarkable roll.

Malcolm heard the "Jocky"—a word he disliked. In ordinary circumstances he would have resented it, perhaps demanded an apology. But the information Lord Barrymore had given him had left his head in a whirl. He looked up quickly, stared a moment, blinking, and then returned to the collection of his winnings. He would depart.

But Lord Barrymore would not permit this.

"Lord, man! If you go before you've finished the cast, they'll know I told you something important!" He was whispering again, very excited, frightened too. "I'm suspect already, and there are spies everywhere. At least finish your cast!"

There was reason in the request. Almost savagely, as though he were attacking an enemy, Malcolm pushed the money to the center of the table and picked up the dice.

The gamesters moved closer. There was a considerable crowd now.

"Seven," called the Young Glenallan.

Six and ace fell. Malcolm wanted only to get away. He called seven again, and cast five and two. Annoyed, he waved a hand to indicate that he would bet all the money on the table.

Fitzstephen asked: "Aren't you getting reckless, Jocky?"

Again that "Jocky." And again that harsh sarcasm, intended for insult. Fitzstephen was in an ugly humor, and he had been drinking. The Young Glenallan looked up sharply. But he told himself that he must not fight now. He was needed elsewhere, in the north.

"All of it," he said, "and this besides." He threw down the money he had been holding in his left hand, a matter of some thirteen or fourteen pounds. It was all he had left in London, and the instant after he had tossed it on the table he realized that he should have held it. If he lost this one cast, he would be obliged to borrow in order to ride post to Scotland; the Northern Diligence would be much too slow. The Stuart would be needing money, too. War was a costly business, and a good subject should not be gambling at such a time.

But the bet was made. Captain Fitzstephen dropped his last shilling, and others covered the rest. The crowd was silent. Even at Martin's you seldom saw that much cash on one table.

"Seven!"

He rolled ten, a difficult point to make. He was angry with himself now. He picked up the dice and cast swiftly, frowning at them as they rattled across the smooth table. Four, six, four, nine. The lace at his sleeves got in his way; impatiently he tucked it back under the broad brown cuffs. He went on rolling. Aces, eight, four—and then two fives.

There was a burst of excited talk. The Young Glenallan quietly pocketed the money and bet five pounds. Somebody at his left covered the bet.

"Seven!"

He threw a nine and then seven, so that the roll was finished at last. The man at his left picked up the ten pounds, and the Young Glenallan turned to leave.

Captain Fitzstephen of the Dragoons was ordinarily an amiable and even a convivial young man. He liked companionship. But money he worshiped. A younger son, with much ambition, he knew that his only chance for military advancement lay in the acquisition of His Majesty's silver, for commissions were being priced higher every year. The Scot's spectacular luck, and the Scot's eagerness to quit the game as soon as his roll was ended, infuriated Fitzstephen. The punch turned sour inside of him.

"Leaving so soon, Jocky?" he asked. "It seems you don't like our company."

Malcolm of Glenallan stuffed the last piece of gold into his waistcoat pocket, and he put his cocked hat under his arm.

"I don't," he said.

Men at this table suddenly lowered their voices, as they raised their eyes.

Malcolm strove to keep cool. He promised himself that he

would not be drawn into a silly and perhaps perilous duel because of the snorting of a drunken fool who couldn't take his losses with grace.

But Fitzstephen, a tall brute, magnificent in his scarlet coat with blue facings and gorgeous gold braid, drained his punch glass deliberately, set it down on the table, and said:

"But you like our money, eh? Yes, all you damned Scotchmen are like that."

Resolutions went for nothing. Malcolm *shouldn't* fight. The flaming cross would be carried through the hills soon, and every true clansman was needed as never before. But "damned Scotchmen" was too much. He took the hat from under his arm and, reaching across the hazard table, struck Captain Fitzstephen squarely in the face.

Instantly there was uproar and confusion. Gentlemen dragged the Young Glenallan back from the table. He had drawn his dress sword, but consented to be held from behind. Other gentlemen, on the opposite side, dragged back a loudly swearing Fitzstephen.

"Damn me, I'll fight him! I'll skewer him! Let me go!"

Men who had been playing whist-and-honors as quietly as you please sprang to their feet and hurried toward this table. The lackeys, obliged to retain their positions at the punch bowls, strained their necks to see over the heads of the gentlemen, and some of them even stood on chairs. One old fellow slapped his hip repeatedly, saying over and over again:

"Damned well done, sir! Egad, that boy has spirit!"

Mr. Martin, the proprietor, hurried in from another room, straightening his cravat as he trotted.

"My lords! Gentlemen! Surely this can be arranged quietly?"

His friends, and notably two fellow officers, were conferring with Captain Fitzstephen, imploring him to be quiet and to settle the matter decently. A tall man, whom Malcolm remembered having met at Vauxhall, though he could not recall to memory his name, offered his services; and Malcolm gladly accepted.

"I don't care what weapons," Malcolm said, "but it must be here and now—anyway it must be tonight."

The tall man attributed this wild talk to excitement. He tut-tutted soothingly, and disappeared.

The crowd stilled somewhat, the loud cries dropping to quick blurred murmurs. In one corner of the Long Room, two lackeys were holding a young buck, very drunk, who had drawn his sword and was announcing his intention of fighting somebody, he didn't care whom. There was no attempt to continue the play. Mr. Martin, bustling here and there, was shoved aside by every man to whom he appealed: there were tears in the old villain's eyes, for a scandal might bring the beaks down upon him.

Malcolm's representative returned, nodding assurance. Everything had been arranged. At the old cockpit in Birdcage Walk. Fitzstephen preferred the small sword.

"It will be too dark there now," said Malcolm.

"Why, you won't fight *now!* We have arranged the meeting for Thursday morning at five o'clock."

The Young Glenallan shook his head.

"I'll fight now or not at all. Tell him that."

Fitzstephen's representatives, having overheard, broke into prompt protests. Their man had been drinking: they would not permit him to go to the field now.

"Listen, I will drink twice what he's had and then meet him. Is that fair?"

There was laughter and a few cries of scorn. The crowd, previously favoring neither man, now quite obviously had turned against the Scot. The proposal was preposterous.

These barbarians should be kept out of establishments for gentlemen. Probably the fellow was a coward, willing to fight the captain while the captain was drunk but afraid to meet him when he was sober.

"Why won't you fight Thursday morning?" somebody asked.

"I can't. I'm leaving London tomorrow morning, early."

"Postpone your departure."

"I can not."

"Is this mission to important?"

"It is."

"Is it more important than your honor, Jocky?" somebody in the back asked.

Somebody else snickered. And the Young Glenallan was suddenly sick of the whole business. On one side there was the Stuart cause. On the other side was his personal honor, yes—but in a dirty gambling-house brawl. His father, his uncles, his grandfather, the MacIldowies of Glenallan for more generations than a clerk could count, had fought for the Stuart kings. Glenallan blood had been shed at Sheriffmuir, at Kilsyth, at Bannockburn, on Flodden Field. . . .

Malcolm hated Englishmen. He had been in London for two years, and every day he spent there had increased his dislike of the place and its people. They were all merchants, the Londoners, or else men with merchants' hearts. Prince Charles would plead in vain for their support. Their fidelity depended upon trade. You could measure their loyalty by the figures in their profit and loss columns.

He owed it to himself to go through with this duel. But he owed it to all his ancestors, and to his rightful king, to quit London without delay and be ready when he and his claymore were called.

One of the captain's representatives confronted him. The crowd hushed to hear this man.

"We have made reasonable arrangements. Your offer is ridiculous. Unless you can give us some explanation of why you are leaving the city so soon, we must assume that you are not willing to go to the field."

Of course he had an explanation; but he could not speak it here.

"Tell your friends," he replied, "that I'm willing to fight him with any weapons and at any place, but the affair must be postponed. I am not at liberty to explain. Tell him I will meet him if I have to cross the world to do it. But the affair *must* be postponed!"

This brought backs. The gamesters had no further use for him. The tall gentleman who had offered his services now asked to be excused. Mr. Martin looked relieved, and, eager to hasten the thing through, he joined his catcalls with those of his patrons.

A lane fell open to the door. Some of the gentlemen made mock bows. Some of them grinned. But most were grave, even threatening, and they indicated plainly to the Young Glenallan that his company was not desired.

He looked around. He had no friend in the place. His anger would make no impression upon these cold exact Englishmen. And he could not possibly explain.

He put his hat under his left arm, and amid a terrific silence, a silence that was to ring in his ears for the rest of his life, he walked across the floor and out into the street.

CHAPTER 2

IT WAS MIDSUMMER, but the London streets, though warm, had a nighttime freshness. Nevertheless, Malcolm's face was hot with anger and shame. He had never known such a rage. He vowed again, inwardly, that when he had seen King

James upon his rightful throne and was free once more to engage in personal quarrels, he would seek out this Captain Fitzstephen if it were necessary to cross the seven seas to do it. He vowed it quietly, by himself, kissing the blade of his dress sword because he had no dagger to kiss.

Fitzstephen's broad, florid face, his arrogant mouth, his narrow brown eyes, were fastened in Malcolm's memory by hooks of hate.

Of course such mental tempests were vain. Better sense told him that he probably would have been killed in the duel anyway. With pistols the result might be doubtful, for Malcolm was a crack shot. But for all the fencing lessons—and a pretty penny they had cost—he still was a poor hand with the small sword. The heavy claymore of his native hills had spoiled him for the handling of these steel toothpicks. He never could remember, in the excitement of a bout, that there was no edge on the thing, but only a point, and he had a risky habit of beating his opponent's blade and so swinging his own point out of line. Yes, in a duel with court swords, Fitzstephen might have killed him. Still, he would rather be killed, even by such a man, than be thought a coward.

He walked rapidly, his long legs swinging. He was impatient of the little, crooked streets. He wanted the brush of heather against his brogues and a kilt flapping at his legs. It was two years since he had been in Scotland. His father had sent him to London "to see what they're like there." He was to make his bow to society, learn to wear the Southron's breeches and fancy silk stockings, and amuse or instruct himself as best he could on an allowance necessarily small.

It was a stupid business at best, and the news that Prince Charles had sailed for the West Coast was doubly welcome to this particular subject.

London was a place for merchants, fops, and women. There was no room to move, no room to walk, and precious little silence. In addition, there was dirt, the necessity of a strained manner, the unavoidable presence of rascals, and an increasing demand upon a gentleman's pocketbook. For it was requisite that he live like a gentleman, even though the name Glenallan meant nothing to these conceited fools.

Malcolm felt very strongly about Englishmen.

Well, there would be an accounting soon. The English had dragged from his throne the rightful Stuart king, the seventh James, and had exiled him, putting a Dutchman and then a stupid drunken German in his place. And James had died in France, and his son, James the Eighth, had remained, a lonesome and neglected monarch, in Italy. But Prince Charles, the Prince of Wales, was coming over now. There would be an accounting.

So ran Malcolm's thoughts as he strode the narrow streets toward the Cardinal's Hat, his inn, on the other side of Clerkenwall Green.

The streets were exceptionally quiet. He passed a chocolate house—a buzz of talk and a glow of light that approached, climaxed, and receded without attention from him. He passed a group of roisterers, bucks out in search of devilment. He passed a dirty, crouched little man, who scurried away as though afraid to face him.

He turned up a dark and narrow alleyway, connecting two somewhat broader but hardly better-lit thoroughfares. And so deep were his thoughts, and so strong his emotions, that it was not until he was halfway up this alley that he realized something was wrong. Those light footsteps had been behind him for several squares. And he looked up to see a solitary figure at the other end of the alley.

This man was a tall, thin silhouette. A light cloak enwrapped him, and his hat was not a tricorn but a broad-brimmed felt, of the sort affected by travelers—and highwaymen. Malcolm turned. Behind him were two men. They approached with a rapid but peculiarly wary gait. Malcolm looked the other way. The solitary silhouette had come to life. He, too, made real by his motion, approached.

This could not be chance. Malcolm was trapped. Both ends of the alley were stopped to him. On either side there were only the high windowless backs of houses, too steep and smooth for climbing.

Cursing quietly, Malcolm put his back against one of the walls in such a manner that the moonlight would be sprayed into the eyes of whoever faced him. He drew.

The three men were before him. The one with the light cloak was masked. There was about this man something of the air of a gentleman, though the others clearly were cutthroats from Whitefriars.

"Let us be quiet about this," said the man with the mask. "You understand, of course, that we want your purse. We will not take your life along with it unless you oblige us to do so."

Stuffed into the lower waistcoat pockets, none too carefully, were the winnings at hazard. The memory of them added to Malcolm's discomforture. Ordinarily, footpads would get from him no more than a few guineas, if they got that much, but this was a fortune he carried tonight.

"I regret the haste, but we are too near the square to risk delay. You must appreciate that, sir."

"I appreciate," said Malcolm, "that you're too near the square to risk a shot. It happens that I have a pistol under my coat here, and unless the three of you are gone instantly, I'll murder a scoundrel and fetch a crowd with one discharge."

The man with the mask was a cool character.

"You are lying," he said. "If you had a pistol, you'd have drawn it to frighten us off, instead of drawing your sword."

"Nevertheless," insisted Malcolm, "you would not dare to shoot me."

"True. But you will observe that my companions, although not exactly Knights of the Garter, are armed with swords, and that I carry such a weapon myself."

It was three to one, then, and the Young Glenallan a wild blade to boot. But he had dodged debate once this night, and he'd be hanged, he told himself, if he dodged it again.

"Perhaps," he suggested coldly, "you and your companions would like to give me an exhibition of your skill?"

"Well said, sir. On guard!"

He drew like a flash, and stepped in. The two villains from Whitefriars, not so courageous and certainly not so skillful, came in also, stiff-armed.

Malcolm took two counters, and raised his voice in a lusty shout for help.

It was three to one. And it would have gone very badly indeed—indeed, it could not have lasted for more than a minute—had Malcolm been silent.

At the upper end of the alley there appeared a group of link boys, and there was a sudden clatter of hoofs.

"Coming! Coming! Hallo!"

Two horsemen galloped down the narrow way, steel out, bodies bent forward.

The highwaymen ran, and the horsemen pursued, and abruptly Malcolm was left alone.

Sword still in hand, he walked to the upper end of the alley where the link boys were. In their midst he found a sedan chair. Of its occupant there was visible only a slim round arm, pink sleeves to the elbow, where triple ruffles of Valenciennes hung.

"May I ask what person it is I have to thank?"

A head appeared—a very beautiful head—with oval face,

and combed-back powdered hair, and a tiny lace cap. The girl smiled in pleased amazement.

"How happy to meet you here, Mr. Glenallan."

He bowed, and kissed the hand she extended.

"Lady Helen! There is no one to whom I'd rather owe my life."

"Was it as bad as that? I'd supposed that some bucks were annoying you."

"No, it was tobymen."

"Then I am glad a thousand times that we took this way home. We've been to a Drury Lane. But you mustn't thank me. It's my brother and Sir John Appleton."

Lady Helen Hornsby was one of the few things that had made London endurable to Malcolm. He had met her frequently at the theater, at Ranelagh, at the Italian Opera House, at Don Saltero's museum in Cheyne Walk. But they had never been intimate. Naturally shy, he was especially so with this lady. She was at the court, attending one of the Germans, and her father was Herbert Viscount Hornsby, whose name was a great one in Whig politics. What would Malcolm have to do with such a woman? Or rather, what would such a woman have to do with Malcolm of Glenallan?

She was tall, slim, brown haired. Perhaps her wealth and position had helped to inspire some of the verses that were heaped at her feet, but no man could deny that Lady Helen alone, had she been a farmer's daughter and penniless, would have drawn the admiration of all who saw her.

Her eyes were blue, or perhaps purple—Malcolm could never be certain, and indeed it was a matter that had puzzled more sophisticated observers. At any rate they were big eyes and very bright. Her nose was tiny; and when she was riding, and not fully powdered, you might discern three or four wee freckles there, the tiniest freckles imaginable. Her mouth was perhaps a shade too long; but Malcolm liked long mouths.

Just now, in a new pink gown, with banded V-front, voluminous side hoops, and turn-back cuffs from under which the Valenciennes cascaded, she was, it seemed to him, almost reprehensibly beautiful. There were crescent patches on her cheeks, and pink satin brocade slippers on her tiny feet. One long curl, perfectly powdered, fell over her right shoulder to the ruffles of the corsage.

"You should go to the theater more often, Mr. Glenallan. If you could have been with us tonight! Mr. Garrick was the Abel Drugger."

Malcolm could not be amused by the strutting of mummers. They only aped the folk he saw around him every day, and those folk he hated. He was not in London, he reasoned, to be wasting money on such fripperies. Instead, he had spent most of his time in the school of pugilism, in Oxford Road near Adam and Eve Court, where he was one of the Great Broughton's most promising pupils; at Foubert's Riding Academy, though he would never, he feared, be a personable horseman; and at the tennis court back of the Haymarket; and also at M. Loti's fencing academy.

But Lady Helen seemed to like the theater, and Malcolm strove to be polite with her.

"I'm sure it was a wonderful play," he said.

"It was magnificent!"

She paused. Perhaps she had been letting her enthusiasm fly too far? She drew herself back abruptly, and asked:

"I suppose there are no theaters in Scotland, Mr. Glenallan?"

It was odd to be called Mr. Glenallan, but that was how everybody in London addressed him. The Young Glenallan meant nothing to them: they could tell at a glance, they'd say, that he was young.

"No. There were some men who wanted to start a theater in Edinburgh, but the clergy were against it."

"Now, that's too bad. What do the people of the village do at night?" And before he could venture an answer she exclaimed: There! I knew there was something I wanted to tell you! As soon as his Majesty goes back to Herrenhausen, and he's going next week—for which thank the Lord, Mr. Glenallan!—why, when he goes Gerald and I are to visit our cousins in Edinburgh. That will interest you."

It did interest him, very much. It seemed also to trouble him. He started to say something, then tightened his lips.

"Tell me—you know, I have never been in Scotland before —tell me, what sort of village is Edinburgh?"

"It's smaller than London," said Malcolm, "but much better."

"Better than London? How?"

"For one thing, the people are decent."

"I'm afraid you're harsh with us, Mr. Glenallan. You don't like London, do you?"

"No."

"Now, you know, Mr. Glenallan, I have Scotch blood myself. Did I ever tell you that?"

She had. Her maternal grandmother was a Grant of Glenmoriston. It was a fact upon which Malcolm loved to dwell.

"Aye," he said. "You told me that."

He was not a boor, though certainly his manners were not the manners to which she was accustomed. It was difficult to make talk with him. She paused again, wondering what to say next, and as she paused the two horsemen returned. They had not been able to catch the robbers.

Malcolm greeted his saviors coolly, though he shook their hands.

"I am your servant, gentlemen," he said.

There was an embarrassing pause. Neither Sir John Appleton nor the Honorable Gerald Hornsby thought highly of Malcolm; and to him they were just another pair of Englishmen, to whom—and he almost regretted it—he owed his life. They did not dismount.

"It was pleasant," Lady Helen ventured, "to have Mr. Glenallan to chat with while you two chased the villains. I've been telling him about the trip we're going to make, Gerald."

"Yes, we're about to visit your country, sir."

"This will be next week?" Malcolm asked.

"As soon as His Majesty departs. Lord, I hope that will be next week! The court, Mr. Glenallan, is the stupidest place in all London."

"Aye."

"Gerald thinks I should feel proud to be a lady-in-waiting. I wish he had to do it. Emily's as gracious as anybody could be, when she's in good humor. But she doesn't like a one of us. We try, but we can't be confidential with her. After all, Mr. Glenallan, she's a German. And it's so difficult to get along with anybody from another nation."

"Aye," said Malcolm heartily.

This made for another awkward silence. Lady Helen was annoyed. But somebody had to make conversation, and Gerald and Sir John were as glum as a pair of porters.

"La, I must be off to bed. The princess is always up at seven. We have to ride in the morning. And later Farinelli's going to sing in Dr. Arne's new opera—what is it called, Gerald?"

"I've forgotten."

"Well, whatever it is, Harriet attended one of the rehearsals yesterday, and she tells me it will be well worth hearing. Won't you go with us, Mr. Glenallan?"

To go to the opera with Lady Helen Hornsby! It would be

a pleasure almost as great as the killing of Captain Fitz-stephen. But Malcolm shook his head.

"I return to Scotland tomorrow."

"Well, sir! We have been talking here for ten minutes, and you didn't tell me that you were leaving London. I trust that no bad news has reached you from home?"

"Not bad news, no."

"Then perhaps we will meet in Scotland? Is your estate near Edinburgh, Mr. Glenallan?"

"No. It is benorth the Great Glen."

"Oh."

"Benorth the Grampians."

"Yes, I had forgotten. You are one of the—of the High-landers, aren't you?"

He nodded.

"One of the Wild Scots," he said. "They call us that," he went on, "to distinguish us from the Lowlanders, who are the Tame Scots—so damned tame that they'll do anything the German tells 'em to."

Lady Helen spoke quickly.

"La, don't start talking politics! When Gerald here gets to talking politics he never stops. It's all I hear at court, and there's nothing bores me so." She signaled to the chairmen and the link boys. "Forgive me if I wearied you with the praises of Mr. Garrick, Mr. Glenallan. For me at least the interruption has been most pleasant. And we'll hope to meet in Edinburgh, eh? Gerald and I will be at John Forbes' house in the Cannongate, whatever that means. Perhaps you will see us there on your way back to London. For you're coming back to London, of course?"

"I hope to come back."

He did not add that he hoped to come as a conqueror for the rightful king, in arms and with his clan at his back.

"Well, good night, sir."

The carriers lifted the chair. But he stepped to the window again.

"Is it necessary that you go next week?"

She was amazed by his earnestness. She covered her confusion with a small laugh.

"Oh, I assure you it is! Gerald and I promised them more than a year ago."

"I would not go, if I was you."

"Why—why, truly, Mr. Glenallan, this is the most extraordinary thing I've ever heard you say! It was you who yammered to me for near an hour—that one night at Lady Hawley's when I did manage to get you to talk—about what a beautiful country Scotland was. And now you advise me not to go there!"

He blushed when she recalled the night he had talked so freely—a wonderful night when, tired of dancing, she had sat with him, fragrant and exquisite, and asked him questions about the Highlands.

"Well, not at this time of the year."

"Why, it was in the spring, you told me, that the countryside was loveliest!"

He fumbled with words, while the Honorable Gerald Hornsby and Sir John Appleton, both puzzled, waited, their reins straight.

"No, not at this time. Only in the very early spring. And Edinburgh is not worth seeing anyway. It is only a city. All cities are ugly."

"I'm afraid you don't want us to go because you may meet us and have to listen to me chatter again about Mr. Garrick. La, she should be politer than that, Mr. Glenallan."

"No, no!" He shook his head desperately. "You must not think that. It gives me pleasure to hear you talk, whatever you say."

The horsemen, in spite of themselves, smiled at a gallantry

so clumsy. Lady Helen smiled too, but it was a gracious, encouraging smile.

"Well, then," she said, "we have all of us been pleased. So now we must be hurrying home, Mr. Glenallan. Good night, sir, and a good trip."

"Good night," he called.

But he stood in the center of the street, shaking his head. She was going to Edinburgh—the first place the Stuart would strike.

CHAPTER 3

THE KNIGHT OF GLENALLAN lay dying, but the boldest man in the world would have hesitated to rile him. His enormous frame, covered by tartan blankets, looked capable of any exertion. He seemed to be the only person in the big room: it was not until Malcolm had been there for ten minutes or longer that he observed the old woman and the old man, bent gillies, by the side of the bed. The chief, gray and grim, monopolized attention.

Many years before, the Parliament, under James VI, had made another determined attempt to break the clan system by passing a law that required every chief to produce legal proof of his ownership of the land he occupied. Now most of the clans had held this land from time beyond count, and nobody, least of all themselves, knew how it had come to them. But by the new law, unless they produced the title deeds, with all the appended stamps and seals and ribbons and such, the property would be confiscated and the gallant gentlemen, whose genealogies nobody dared to question, would be penniless wanderers.

The king's officers had appeared at Allan's Castle then and said to the MacIldowie of the time:

"Where is your title deed?"

And the MacIldowie had drawn his two-edged broadsword, his mighty claymore.

"Here is my title deed!"

It was of this stuff that Sir Douglas was made. He was a throwback to the days when any man was a gentleman who would kill any man who said he wasn't; when clerks and barristers were servants to be summoned for the writing of a letter or the framing of a proclamation, not pompous asses who strutted in laces and silks, making laws to which brave fellows must submit.

Malcolm knelt before his father not simply because of their relationship but also because the Knight of Glenallan, besides being his father, was his chief.

"My greetings, sir."

The knight took half a bottle of claret from the stool beside the bed, drank deeply, and passed it to his son. Malcolm too had a deep drink, so that between them they emptied the bottle.

"Bring more," said the laird; and the old woman shuffled out.

Then the chief looked long and hard at his older son. His eyes displayed none of the joy he felt; they were, instead, hard and cruelly critical; but in the end he seemed pleased, for he nodded and almost smiled.

"Did you like London?"

"No."

The old man nodded again. The answer did not seem to astonish him.

"I didna like it mysel'. Ye'll no' go back, then?"

"Aye."

"Ye'll go back?"

"Aye, with the men."

"Wi' what men, Callum?"

The old gillie by the side of the bed was evincing alarm. He made frantic motions toward the Young Glenallan, putting a forefinger over his mouth to indicate silence. But Malcolm thought that his father should know whatever there was to know.

"Did they not tell you, then?"

"Tell me what, Callum?"

"Prince Charles, Jamie's son, has sailed from France. He will be landing soon, somewhere in the Macleod country."

The laird sat up. His eyes all but popped out of his great shaggy head; his voice quavered; his hand trembled.

"You're sure of that, Callum? 'Tis no' a wild tale?"

"My Lord Barrymore told me in London, and the Cameron of Fassden when I was coming here. It's why I came back."

The laird relaxed. If a Cameron had said it, it was true.

Then he remembered something, and looked up suddenly. The gillie crouched to the floor like a mongrel that awaits the whip.

"*You knew!*"

The gillie nodded, wetting his lips.

"Ye war sae weak, Macdomhnull Dhu. We didna dare—"

Sir Douglas fairly quivered. He almost managed to get out of bed.

"*Weak*—ye filthy dog!"

The gillie ran from the room. Sir Douglas addressed his son, pointing after the man.

"Kick him! Throw him out o' the glen! It's no' a helot o' mine would be such as him!"

Malcolm nodded, and walked rapidly out into a long stone corridor, high arched and absolutely bare, musty with old air and black with the very pressure of time against its walls.

"An' bring more wine back wi' ye," Sir Douglas called after him.

Malcolm came to a little serving room in which he found the two gillies. They threw themselves on their knees before him, imploring him to be merciful.

"Get up, you fools. You should have told him. Bring me six bottles of claret. And you, Patty, where is my brother?"

"I' the hall he be, Macdomhnull Dhu. I'll be—"

"Don't bother. I'll go to him."

Malcolm hurried down another corridor, a higher corridor, and entered the banquet hall of Allan's Castle. It was a huge place, lighted only by a couple of bogpine torches and a fire of peat in the fireplace, for there were no windows. The ceiling was not even visible, so thick were the shadows. The walls were hung with ancient weapons—pikes, claymores, dirks, tasseled halberds, longbows, crossbows, maces—and with dusty, rusty pieces of armor—shirts of reticulated mail, pennyplate camails, habergeons, conical helmets.

Before the fire stood Fergus MacIldowie. He was a slim, smooth-muscled lad, straight and handsome, nervous in his movements, dark, boyish. He was eight years younger than Malcolm, and lacked perhaps that stern insistence upon military etiquette, that somber sense of hard duty, that his brother had inherited from Sir Douglas.

"Tell me about London, Callum. Is it a braw town, as they say?"

"Hush, ladie! And your father dying in the next chamber! London is all dirt and noise."

"They're waiting out there for you, Callum. Walter MacPhail and Evan, too."

"They must wait. And let you and Gillie Angus be here, where I can call you. There's death coming, Fergus—and after death, war."

He returned to the bedchamber, carrying wine. The stones of Allan's Castle, above him, below and all around him, were good to feel and see and smell.

The bedroom was gloomy. Night had come, and through two high narrow windows he could see the tiny stars. The fire burned stodgily. Malcolm lighted a candle by the bed, but this gave only the thinnest sort of glow, as though it were afraid to blaze in full—afraid, perhaps, of the gaunt old laird.

Malcolm opened two bottles and each man took one.

"*Deoch slaint an Righ*," said the MacIldowie, raising his bottle.

"*Deoch slaint an Righ*—God save the King."

They drank deep. The laird retained his bottle afterward, shaking his head impatiently when Malcolm would have taken it from him to put it on the floor.

"Now, tell me about Charlie."

He listened carefully. He shook his head when Malcolm told him of the nature of the Jacobites in London.

"Aye, they're a worthless lot there. It will come frae the Highlands, Callum."

"Aye, frae the Highlands."

"An' I'm no' too sure o' the man here either, ye ken? They're a pack o' farmers these days. The MacGregors will turn out, that's certain. An' Clanranald, an' Keppoch, an' the MacIan o' Glencoe. . . . If Lochiel was here we could be sure o' him, but he's an old man in France, ye ken, and he dinna dare come back if he would. Will the Young Cameron fight?"

"Donald? Aye, he'll fight."

The laird continued thoughtfully, counting on his fingers the clans upon which it was certain, he believed, that the Stuart could count. The Macleods of Harris, the Macleods of Barra, the Stewarts of Appine, Cluny Macpherson's men, the Kinloch-Moidart Macdonalds . . .

"Fergus must no' be out," he commanded. "In the Fifteen, ye ken, we near lost the glen?"

Malcolm remembered the story. His uncles had been

killed in battle, his grandfather captured, tried, convicted, and with great solemnity hanged and quartered. His father had been obliged to fly to France, in company with other Highland gentlemen. Glenallan, confiscated by the crown, had been bought up by a Lowlander, who moved into Allan's Castle, very pleased to find himself a lord of land.

The Lowlander had been quickly disillusioned. The Cameron country was adjacent, and the Lochiels and the MacIldowies were cousins. That Lowlander's cattle began to disappear, and his collies, and his fowl, and his very servants—all disappeared. In the second week he himself rode forth to look over the ground. His damned Lowland bonnet had been shot off his head and his horse had been killed beneath him. After this he had returned to the city and sold the property. A Cameron had purchased it, indirectly, and thus Glenallan had returned to the descendants of Domhnull Dhu.

But the lesson had been learned. One male member of the family must stay at home in the war to come, and the land must be held in his name; for there were title deeds and all that now.

"I suppose they'll march on Edinburgh first?"

"Aye."

The laird took another deep drink. Malcolm opened a third bottle. The firelight, very faint, and the candlelight, fainter still, flickered weirdly on the high black walls and the faraway ceiling. The shadows twisted into little corners or squirmed as though they were wounded. The floor lay blank and blandly staring—yellow near the chimneyplace and sliding into deep orange against the far wall. Sometimes from other parts of the castle there came the sound of a door shut carefully, or the sobs of a gillie who wept because his master was dying, or the growl of a restless dog. But mostly it was quiet.

"Call Fergus," the laird said suddenly. He had not spoken for more than an hour.

Malcolm passed under the high doorway, down the corridor, through the serving room and into the banquet hall. His face was stiff with grief, and there were tears in his eyes. It was an awful thing to think that such a man must die.

Fergus was asleep in a chair. Gillie Angus stood behind him, in attendance. Back among the shadows, Evan of Lochallan, gentleman of the clan, and Walter MacPhail, *am Fear Sporain*, were talking quietly. Malcolm only nodded to Evan and MacPhail, for, though the sight of them pleasured him after these years, it was no time for social talk. He awakened his brother, and without a word they went to the bedchamber.

Fergus knelt before his father. Fergus, like Malcolm, feared this man and respected him, and loved him, too.

"It will be the *deoch* and *doris*, laddies."

He raised his bottle. The sons took bottles and raised these, waiting for the toast.

"Callum, you will carry my claymore." The laird's voice was very weak; he was holding his arm up only by a terrible exertion of strength. "Gentlemen, *Deoch slaint an Righ!*"

"*Deoch slaint an Righ!*"

They drank, and immediately afterward the Laird of Glenallan dropped his bottle, and his eyes closed and the muscles of his face went limp. He did not speak or move again. Within ten minutes of that drink he was dead.

CHAPTER 4

It was the first time in more than twenty-five years that the chief of the Glenallans had summoned the clansmen to war. There were not many of them, fewer than ever; yet no detail was omitted from the ceremony, for the new chief was a stickler for etiquette.

He stood on a mound just outside the castle gates—very young, very tall and solemn. He was dressed in the *braecan feile,* or belted plaid. The family tartan was red and blue and yellow and black, a vivid, unforgettable mixture. The plaid fell, nicely pleated, almost to his kneecaps, and in the rear it was lifted up loosely and brought over to the left shoulder, being fastened in front by a pewter brooch; and it belled out behind him in the breeze.

Malcolm wore a bright blue coat, very short, with broad cuffs turned over with scarlet, and a scarlet waistcoat. His hose were stretched over the thick muscles of his lower legs, and were held by yellow garters from which yellow ribbons fell. He wore soft brogues, a plain doeskin sporran with pewter check top, and a narrow white stock. On his head was a blue bonnet, to which had been fastened a small white cockade.

There were also on the bonnet three long eagle feathers, which showed that he was a full chief who owed allegiance only to his king.

But it was the weapons Malcolm carried that pleased the clansmen most. The MacIldowies always had been poor; but there was nobody better armed. In Malcolm's right hand, the stock resting on the ground, was a long musket, newly come from France, very straight. His left hand gripped the hilt of his claymore. This was a genuine Andrea Ferrara—long, heavy, double-edged, with a high median ridge, and scarlet velvet pading in the basket hilt. It had been carried by the chief of the clan for almost three hundred years, and it was as bright now, and as sharp, as the day when it had come from the Spaniard's famous forge.

In addition, Malcolm was equipped with three dirks, triangular, single-edged, and very sharp. One was in a sheath in the back of his round leather target; one was suspended from his belt, on the right side; and the third was thrust into the stocking on his right leg. A very broad belt, made of black leather, encircled his waist; another belt, equally broad, went over his right shoulder to join its brother before and behind; and to this upper belt were attached two Doune pistols with silver mountings adroitly scrolled.

It may be understood, then, that Malcolm MacIldowie Macdomhnull Dhu, the Laird of Glenallan and chief of the clan of that ilk, was a person any Highlander would be proud to follow.

"Blow up, Angus!"

Old Angus was the hereditary clan piper, who had been out with Malcolm's father at Sheriffmuir and Glenshiel. He was very old, and walked with uncertain step, but he had learned his art on the Isle of Skye and could pipe like a MacCrimmon inspired. He was called Old Angus to distinguish him from Gillie Angus, who attended the new chief.

Soon the loud notes flew, and the peaks threw them back, and the valleys and ravines gave them gleeful harbor. Old Angus played the *Cruinneachadh nan Ailein,* ancient rallying-song of the clan.

Now two men, who had been standing rather apart from the others on the edge of the mound, strode forward to join the chief.

One was young, slim, and of medium height. He was a handsome fellow, dressed almost as elaborately as Malcolm himself, at whose right side he now stood. He was Evan of Lochallan, who owed homage to the Glenallan by reason of a grant at the western end of the glen—a grant the Lochallans had ruled for many years.

The older man was middle-aged, rather stout, stolid, with a red face, thick wrists, large hands and feet. He was Walter

MacPhail, another grantee, of lesser family. He took his position at the chief's left side.

These were the only two gentlemen of the clan who were of the age to go to war.

The helots followed. Gillie Angus came first, by reason of his position as valet of the chief. Then the three sons of Mac-Michael Roy—Great Davie, a monstrous fellow, the only man in the West Country who could throw the caber farther than Malcolm; and John and Paul. Then came Lochallan's gillie, a very old man who was also named John. And finally there came a vacant-faced, short, waddling fellow whose name nobody seemed to know but who was always called Dafty. Dafty had been accepted into the clan by Sir Douglas, who made the fellow his innocent, or jester, a position the poor halfwit could fill only nominally, for he had no ability to make songs or to dance, and indeed rarely moved except at command.

These, then, were the warriors of the Clan Glenallan, all the men that Malcolm could bring into the field.

The villagers were grouped in a half-circle, facing this mobilization, on slightly lower ground. There were perhaps thirty of them—women and children, and men so old that they could scarcely stand. Most of them wept, though less from grief than from envy.

The song was finished. Old Angus, chest heaving, face sweaty, but with a smile of pride, slung the bagpipes over his shoulder and stepped back with the rest of the commoners.

Malcolm turned to face them.

"His Majesty, King James, King of Scotland, England, and Ireland, has sent his oldest son, the Prince of Wales, to raise the faithful clans. Prince Charles has been created Prince Regent. That means he is like the king. He is your lord above

me. I will read the proclamation issued by His Gracious
Majesty King James—"

He did so, loudly, slowly, gravely, stumbling over some of
the long words, and frowning upon the paper that he had
drawn from a pocket of his waistcoat. Evan of Lochallan
listened with wide gray eyes, fully alive to the importance of
the occasion. Walter MacPhail, who had read the proclamation previously, was quiet and perhaps a bit bored. The
helots stared attentively. They didn't understand a word of
it, for the proclamation was in English, but they listened because it was their duty to listen when their chief spoke.

Malcolm finished, folded the paper, and put it back into
his pocket. He cleared his throat.

It was a dark wet morning. The rain was like a fine spray
from the sea; the mist was thick upon the hills. A breeze
carried past them, toward the grim old towers of Allan's
Castle, where it moaned ghoulishly.

"And so we are going away," he said, speaking now in the
Gaelic. "Very soon, I think, there will be fighting. There may
be a great deal of fighting before we get King James back
on his throne again—but we will get him there!"

They cheered, for this seemed to them the most eloquent
speech ever given anywhere by any man. They threw their
bonnets into the air.

"Glenallan! Glenallan!"

Malcolm raised his hand for silence.

"Yelling is one thing, fighting another," he said. "Save your
lungs for the battle cries you'll soon be giving. And now—
make your farewells."

He turned aside to speak to Fergus, a jumpy flame of impatience, tears of mortification in his eyes.

"One of us must stay alive," Malcolm had said. The title
deed had been made in the younger brother's name, a clerk
from Fassfern arranging it all. Fergus would be sole authority

in the glen, ruling everybody there. But he had only his own claymore. Every fowling piece and Lochaber ax and pistol had been appropriated for the warrior clansmen. So Malcolm warned him.

"Ye ken, I may not be coming back. It may be redcoats instead."

"I'll know how to meet 'em!"

"Tut, tut. Remember that the name must stay, Fergus. If I'm killed, you'll be the last Glenallan left alive. Don't resist them." He grabbed the boy's shoulder. "Keep the glen, Fergus! There'll be a time enough for vengeance later! Promise me that!"

Fergus nodded. But he bit his lip to control the tremble, and his eyes were cast down.

"I'll not be writing to you, Fergus. Ye ken how I hate to write. Keep the old gillie making trips to Lochiel and Fassfern, and you'll learn more than I could be telling you in a letter. Good-bye."

They shook hands; and Malcolm returned to the center of the mound, where he nodded to Old Angus.

"Blow up."

The men fell into their proper places behind the chief, and they marched over the south hills toward the meeting place. Once only did Malcolm turn to look back. That was atop a rise that would shut the glen from sight, perhaps forever. Allan's Castle, small, brown, awkward, sat firmly, defiantly, on the edge of the tiny bright loch at the other end of the glen. There was nothing soft about it, no decoration, no grass or flowers. It was harsh and bitter, and Malcolm loved it.

The clear cold loch, unruffled by the wind, heedless of the rain, glittered like a steel shield; the brown-and-red hills, shaggy with mossless rocks and with heather, pushed down from three sides, but Allan's Castle would not budge for any of them. Malcolm could see, dimly through the rain and mist, the villagers before the castle gates. He could see Fergus standing there, alone and apart, his plaid ballooning behind him, his right arm raised in a gesture of farewell.

Charles Edward Louis Philip Casimer Stuart stood at the head of River Finnan and stared up a blank, chill glen. The wind moaned, and the water scampered among the rocks as though eager to get out of this dreary place; but these were the only sounds.

Halfway up a hillside, in the direction of Glenakadale's estate, a tiny group of fisherfolk were huddled together like frightened animals, gaping at the newcomers; and near a mound at the lower end of the loch were nine or ten Wild Scots, most of them barefooted but all of them armed. These were the only persons in the glen, after the prince's party. An ungainly black cormorant wheeled in wide circles overhead.

"Why, there's nobody here!"

"It's early, Your Highness. They will come."

Charles Edward Stuart was not so confident. He maintained a smiling face, conscious that his personal charm could be made to count; but he was troubled. These men were his father's subjects, and they should be here. He had summoned them. He had entertained many of the chiefs aboard ship, feeding them wheat bread, main bread, gingerbread, partridge, venison, capon, mutton, goose, drake, capercaillies, not to mention beer, ale, whisky, claret, malvasia, brandy, hippocras, muscatel, usquebaugh. . . . They had promised to meet at Glenfinnan this morning, bringing their men. And—where were they?

For the first time since he had landed, with seven courtiers at his back, to conquer England and Scotland and Ireland, he began to suspect that he might have been betrayed.

This silence, the dreariness and emptiness of the glen, were ominous. But he smiled brightly.

"Of course they will come," he said. "We are early, gentlemen." He held his left hand on the hilt of his sword, while his right hand toyed with the Star of St. Andrew brilliant on his breast. "See who those men are, Buchanan. I don't like their appearance."

Buchanan hurried ahead, to talk a little with the leader of the group at the edge of the loch. Meanwhile, old Tullibardine, leaning on a cane and peering eagerly, had identified the tartan.

"They are Glenallans, Your Highness."

"Is Sir Douglas among them?"

Tullibardine shook his head. He had been exiled for many years, but he knew that he would still recognize Sir Douglas MacIldowie if he saw him; and Sir Douglas, he reported, was not there.

"But the tall laddie wears three feathers in his bonnet."

"Which means?"

"That he's a chief. I don't understand it, Your Highness. But it looks like a MacIldowie. Perhaps he would be one of the Glenallan's sons. They were mere bairns when I went away from here."

Buchanan returned to confirm this, announcing Malcolm MacIldowie MacDomhnull Dhu of Glenallan, with his men.

So Malcolm knelt before the Young Stuart. He knelt before a tall, firmly built man exactly his own age, twenty-four; a man with long muscular arms, broad shoulders, narrow hips, the legs of a runner, and with a high round nose, small mouth, small pointed chin, and large, light-blue eyes that were sometimes hazel.

The prince commanded him, almost immediately, to rise.

"One of the names I was first taught to love and respect," he said slowly, "was that of Glenallan. Your family, sir, has

given my ancestors some of their loyalest subjects. My father,
His Majesty King James, will not forget what you have done.
Nor will I."

Malcolm bowed, embarrassed.

"I am aware," the prince went on, glancing over Malcolm's shoulder at the Glenallans assembled, "that your clan
is a small one. But I am also aware—and I tell you it was my
own royal father who informed me of this—that it is a clan
before whose righteous rage brave men might well tremble."

This did not seem sensible to Malcolm. Brave men do not
tremble. But it was evidently the way they talked in courts.
He bowed again. And the silence that followed suggested to
him that now, at least, he was expected to say something.

"It has fought in the past, Your Royal Highness, and I
hope it will fight again in the very near future."

"I hope it will not be obliged to, Glenallan. I hope that
my father's subjects will see the light when we go among
them, and will expel the German usurper. But—do you speak
for your father, the chief?"

"Your Highness, my father died Wednesday night. I am
the chief now."

Instantly, Charles Edward seized his hand and pressed it.

"I am sorry! Believe me, I am sorry to hear this. I have
heard many tales of your father, and in each of them he was
a gallant gentleman, a loyal subject, and a true descendant of
Donald the Black. There was no man my father loved more.
It will distress him to hear this news."

Malcolm could scarcely believe his ears. The Prince of
Wales, brought up in faraway Italy, had heard of Sir Douglas
of Glenallan, and knew that he was a descendant of Domhnull Dhu! Malcolm was glad that he was not called upon to
speak at that moment, for the lump in his throat was large.

"And I am doubly grateful to you, sir, who have shown
yourself a worthy son by pushing aside the deep grief that

must be yours and offering some of your men to my cause. Believe me, this will not be forgotten."

His head cocked, as though listening for the skirl of the pipes, he studied the hills. Rain blew into his face. He all but sighed.

"You are here early, Glenallan."

"Your Highness, we have been here all night."

"Do you know, Glenallan, that you are the first chief to answer the call. But—where are the rest of your men?"

"There are no more, Your Highness."

"These are all?"

"These are all. We are a very small clan, sir."

The invader managed another smile.

"The more reason for praise, Glenallan. We may need every fighting man we can get, and I knew that we could depend upon the family of MacIldowie. But tell me: when you were coming here, did you see any other clansmen in arms and on the march?"

"None, Sire."

The tops of the hills that hemmed Glenfinnan were scarcely to be seen, for the rain. Yet the sun was struggling to get through. It might yet clear.

"The Cameron country is near here, isn't it, Glenallan?"

"Aye."

"And Lochiel's seat?"

"It is not far."

"Lochiel promised me to have his men here soon after dawn."

"Then he will come, Sire."

"But if you did not see them—"

"If Donald says he'll come, he'll come."

The prince glanced sharply at this tall young chief. But it was no time to resent small impertinences. He smiled instead.

"You are close to the Young Lochiel?" he asked.

"Aye."

"Of course. You are neighbors. Cousins, too, I believe?"

Malcolm explained the exact relationship of the two families. This required a long discourse, for it was very complicated, but the prince listened patiently. Afterward Malcolm asked if he might present the gentlemen he had brought with him; and Charles Edward, though somewhat startled to learn that the ragged group included any gentlemen, nodded permission. Lochallan and MacPhail, then, were called into the presence, and Malcolm, as was only proper, recited the genealogy of each. This again took a long time. The visitor, during it, had a hard time to keep his gaze from the hills.

Malcolm went further. He explained the hereditary privileges and functions of the men under his command. Lochallan was *marischal tighe*, or seneschal, of the chief's household; MacPhail was *am fear sporain*, the treasurer; and Dafty was the jester, *an cleasaiche;* while Great Davie was *an gille mor*, whose duty it was to carry the chief's helmet when there was no fighting.

"But men don't wear helmets today, Glenallan!"

"Your Highness, the office continues. And Great Davie is entitled to precedence over the other gillies just because he holds it."

"And what's all that metal he carries now? Does he take his position so seriously that he polishes up old breastplates and brings them anyway?"

"That is my family's silver, Sire. What's left of it. For the cause."

Real tears came to the prince's eyes then, and he forgot the bare hills and looked instead at this chief with a new respect.

"Now, by God, Glenallan, such devotion mustn't go unrewarded. Kneel down."

Puzzled, Malcolm dropped again to one knee. He felt

something on his shoulder—not a tap either, but a good, firm, friendly blow.

"Rise, Sir Malcolm."

Dazed, gasping, probably looking foolish, he got to his feet. The prince was putting his sword back into its scabbard, and behind him the gentlemen were all beaming and nodding congratulations. Malcolm did not know what to say.

The sound of pipes saved him. The wind had shifted slightly and was coming from the north now, so that the sound reached them suddenly in Glenfinnan. Every head was lifted, every pair of eyes was turned toward the hills in the direction of Lochiel.

"What would that air be, Glenallan?"

"The pibroch of Donald the Black, Your Highness. It is called *Piobaireachd Domhnull Dhu,* and it is the marching song of the Camerons."

"Ah, then Lochiel *is* coming!"

"He told me he would come," Sir Malcolm said.

The sun had made its breakthrough, scattering clouds, and a few minutes later the brow of the hill was bright with clansmen who marched eight abreast, sporrans swinging, claymore hilts atwinkle. In the van were the pipers, blowing up bravely. Behind them, surrounded by his gentlemen and followed by all his warriors, eight hundred strong, walked the Young Lochiel. They marched well, and they sang as they came.

And Malcolm knew now that it was to be a fight to the finish. For Donald of Lochiel was that kind of man.

CHAPTER 5

IN EDINBURGH THERE WAS consternation. All sorts of wild tales went around. The Young Pretender had ten thousand men behind him, twenty thousand, fifty, a hundred. No prisoners would be taken. Houses were to be burned, women and children murdered.

Others tut-tutted the whole thing. The Stuarts and their claims were a dead issue. France would not dare to support such an enterprise: France needed all the money and all the men she could keep at home. And as for Spain, Spain had had her fingers burned once: she would not go near the fire again. What did that leave? Only the Highlanders themselves—a gibbering, jabbering pack of savages. Even supposing that an army—if you could call that rabble an army— could fight without cavalry—even supposing *that*, how could it fight without artillery? The suggestion was absurd. Two hundred of the king's disciplined troops would send the damned rebels scampering back into their hills as fast as their bare feet would carry them.

Nevertheless, there was consternation in Edinburgh. Memories persisted, and from ancient times the people had heard stories of the Wild Scots and their terrible broadswords.

Lady Helen Hornsby listened to all that was said on both sides. She began to understand, now, Mr. Glenallan's reason for quitting London in such haste, and his perturbation when he learned that she was going to Edinburgh. She began to understand why he had refused to fight Captain Fitz- stephen, and she marveled that a man could be so pas- sionately attached to a cause so dubious—to what, indeed, seemed to her a forlorn hope.

Also, she wondered how Mr. Glenallan would look in one of those skirts.

Once, rather half-heartedly, she suggested that they cut short their visit; but Gerald, who was in a towering rage about the whole rebellion, would not consider it.

"We are peaceful, decent subjects of King George," he cried with wholly unnecessary vehemence, "and we will stay right where we are! Let any damned mountaineer try to harm us!"

So Lady Helen had let that subject drop. Anyway, she had heard that the king and queen were making plans to hasten back to London; so probably she would be summoned to court again soon, which would, she hoped, put an end to Gerald's splutterings.

She was seeing a great deal of Captain Fitzstephen, who was stationed with his company just outside the city. The captain annoyed her. He was a handsome man, and among men he appeared to be well liked. Probably he was a good soldier. Certainly he was entertaining and amiable. But whenever he protested that he loved her she could see in his eyes—and so clearly!—the reflection of moneybags. From her point of view, he was altogether too obvious.

Moreover, Gerald, a notorious bungler in such matters, was forever speaking well of Fitzstephen in his sister's presence, with the only-too-apparent purpose of turning her in his favor; and this in itself was enough to decide any spirited young lady against a suitor.

It was Fitzstephen who brought them the most reliable news of the uprising, the official military reports. Even these were vague and brief.

Sir John Cope, as everyone knew, had marched north with three thousand men. But Sir John, the captain informed them one September day, had been outpaced.

"He's a stupid old ass," Fitzstephen explained. "He made a straight line for Fort Augustus, but the rebels fortified a place called Corryarick, and he didn't dare to pass. There he was. He might have come back, or he might have turned toward the coast, or he might have stayed where he was, looking foolish. He turned toward the coast. I suppose that was really the best thing. But the rebels marched right past him, as soon as he'd turned, and now they're on the south of him, coming this way."

"That means they'll attack Edinburgh?" cried Gerald.

"If they ever get here."

"But—who will engage them?"

"Why, we will," Fitzstephen replied. "There are two regiments of dragoons here. These rebels are nothing but shepherds with clubs. Indeed," he added, "I'm really pleased that they slipped past Johnny Cope. It gives us a chance to chase them. And there's a reward of thirty thousand pounds on the Young Pretender's head. Had you heard that?"

The terrible stories multiplied. Merchants were taking their money from the banks and hiding it in their cellars. Clergymen, aquake under the shadow of Rome, were laying plans to visit friends in England, meanwhile exhorting their flocks to stay firm. The trained-bands were drilling night and day, with antiquated fowling pieces, and keeping very bad step indeed.

"It would be easy for me to get passports for both of you," their host told Lady Helen and the Honorable Gerald Hornsby. But Gerald banged his right fist into his left palm, and replied that he'd be doubly damned if any slave of the Pope was going to scare him into quitting the city. And Lady Helen remained discreetly silent.

The Young Pretender had taken Perth. Well, the dragoons and the trained-bands would cock up his beaver, just give them time! Any fool might take Perth. But Edinburgh, with its wall, was another matter. The blue blanket was hoisted on St. Giles' steeple. The town council was in session all day, every day. There was vast excitement in the air.

It was near time for the sun to be coming back, when they reached the Borough Muir and hid themselves in the bushes.

There were nine hundred of them. The space between the

shrubbery where they crouched and the Netherbow Gate—a good hundred and fifty yards—was brilliantly lighted by the moon, and as bare as a monk's pate. There were two sentries at the gate and there were sentries at regular intervals along the wall top. The Highlanders could see these men, fantastic figures, perfectly silhouetted, moving back and forth like pieces of black pasteboard against a gray-green wall.

"Do y'ken the city?" Malcolm asked of Evan Macgregor, younger son of the Macgregor of Glencairnaig.

"Aye."

"Do y'ken whereabout Robert Forbes' house would be?"

"Aye. Near the palace, a grand brown building on the right side of the hill as you go down."

Donald of Lochiel, in charge of the party, had paused, troubled. His orders were to take the city as quietly and with as little bloodshed as possible. His plan now—the only one he could evolve—was for all of the men to rise at a given signal, shrieking their various war cries, brandishing their weapons. They would make a rush for the gate.

Perhaps the sentries, frightened, would forget to shoot. One group of Highlandmen would pretend to make an attempt to scale the wall on the left of the gate, a second group would do the same on the right, while a third and much smaller party would plant a barrel of gunpowder at the gate itself and touch this off—after which all of the men would rush through the breach created. They had brought the gunpowder with them.

But it was a doubtful business. Troubled, the Young Lochiel begged those about him to search their wits for a better plan, the need for speed being apparent in the dawning sky.

"There is nothing else," Mr. Secretary Murray said impatiently.

Donald of Lochiel nodded, sighed, and turned to big Robert MacUalrig, his foster-brother.

"Will you instruct the men, Bobbie? And you, gentlemen, will you instruct your men, please? The signal will be a shot."

He drew one of his pistols—a Spanish weapon with silver mountings, exquisitely chased. He waited while the word was passed among the hidden men. But he shook his head.

The moon, round and very thin, a wafer, slid along through the gray-green sky. Soon it would be gone, and the sun would be fully up.

"Everything is ready," Keppoch reported.

Malcolm and Ardshiel and the faithful MacUalrig nodded: all of the men were prepared for the dash. Lochiel raised his pistol.

"A bottle of brandy I beat you to the gate," Evan Macgregor whispered to Malcolm.

"Accepted, sir."

But Donald of Lochiel had lowered the weapon. For at this very moment, as though answering to a stage cue, the hinges of the Netherbow Gate were heard to creak, and the huge portals started to swing open.

A hackney coach, forbidden by municipal ordinance to remain in the city all night, was returning to Cannongate.

"Leave the gunpowder," whispered Mr. Secretary Murray quickly. "We'll run for it. All of us. No yells."

"Aye," said Donald; and the chieftains passed the new instructions rapidly. The signal was to be "King James the Eighth," spoken by the leader.

The gates swung fully open. The hackney coach, pulled by a beast that had been overworked, started slowly forward. The Highlandmen, grinning, waited. And when the sentries inside the gate itself were hidden by the coach, Donald of Lochiel spoke the signal.

Malcolm got off to a good start, and for half the distance

was running even with Macgregor. He had no sense of fear. A footrace he had always loved, and he was a grand runner. The wager of a bottle of brandy had done much to make the business seem more like a sport—a bit of deviltry that boys might commit—than the capture of a nation's capital.

The driver of the coach, nine-tenths asleep, suddenly stiffened in his seat. He had been looking out over a bare, bleak moor. And this had become, in the time it takes to blink, a mass of half-naked men who flourished swords over their heads and held round targets before them—men with bright skirts and swinging tasseled sporrans. He gasped. He shut his eyes, opened them again. The men were upon him —they were all around him. Two youths dashed past first, and then the gateway was swarming with kilted figures. The reins fell from his hands. He was incapable of any action then.

No less amazed were the sentries. The first man to reach the gate, Evan Macgregor, knocked one of them down with the flat of his claymore. The second, Malcolm of Glenallan, covered two others with his pistols.

"Drop your guns!"

The sentries obeyed, blinking, gasping. And the next instant there were Highlanders everywhere.

"The guardhouse is over this way," Macgregor yelled.

They followed him. Two dozen members of Edinburgh's trained-bands surrendered without the slightest struggle, convinced that all the Wild Scots in the world were confronting them. The sentries above, along the wall top, each made the focus of five or six muskets, were equally submissive. Under Keppoch and Glenallan, one-half of the force made a complete circuit of the walls. Out of sight of the Netherbow Gate, not a single sentry was found who had even been aware of what happened.

The thing had been done with a swiftness and regularity

that was almost military. It was almost as though it had been an exercise previously rehearsed by both parties.

The capital had been captured without the firing of a shot.

CHAPTER 6

THOSE WHO LIVED IN Robert Forbes' house were as amazed as any other in Edinburgh when they woke to learn that the Highlanders had the city. Lady Helen and her host and hostess took it calmly enough, but Gerald was furious.

"Where's Cope?" Gerald demanded. "Where are the militia?"

Neither question, it seemed, could be answered.

"Damn them! No, I don't want breakfast! Forgive me, Forbes, really, but I'm so damned sore—"

The kilted Scots made no try to storm the castle. Instead they walked about in little groups, grinning or gaping at what they saw, chatting among themselves in their outlandish tongue, but disturbing little. Later in the day they began to disappear; and the rumor flew that the Young Pretender was about to make his entry.

"I'm going to watch," Lady Helen told her brother. "I don't care how you feel. *Looking* at him can't do any harm."

There came the sound of Highland pipes, an imperative, imperious, high squeal.

Lady Helen, and Gerald too, together with their cousins and all the servants, crammed the Cannongate windows to watch the parade.

A grand sight! The prince's army had been called a rabble. It was that—and yet it was an army. The men seldom walked in step, but they had a certain system, each clansman, it would appear, knowing what place he should occupy in relation to his chief or chieftain. Many were barelegged;

others wore woggans, stockings without feet; but most of them were shod in brogues, crude shoes made of hide turned inside-out. The gentles were armed to the teeth, more weapons than ten Englishmen would ordinarily tote. The commoners had axes or broadswords, some even mere clubs.

There were not eight thousand of these men, as had been reported by even the more conservative folk in Edinburgh so late as the previous day. There were scarcely half that many. But they were a spirited and formidable lot.

There was the Marquis of Tullibardine, who had seized his brother's estate at Blair and had proclaimed himself Duke of Athole. He rode in a coach drawn by six Flemish mares. His men marched behind him.

There was Oliphant, Laird of Gask; Mercer, Laird of Aldie; Lord Nairn and his followers; doughty old Arthur Elphinstone in his "damnation regimentals," sharing command of a ridiculously small company of cavalry with Lord Kilmarnock and Lord Pitsligo. There was the young Duke of Perth, his head high, eyes flashing. There was Lord George Murray, tall, serious, an expert in military matters: he was Tullibardine's younger brother.

Strangest and most terrible of all were the Highlanders, the true Wild Scots.

There were the Robertsons, from Struan, from Blairfitty, from Cushieval, waving exuberantly at those who watched the parade—the Robertsons, with their dark tartan and their swinging leather sporrans.

There were, of course, many Macdonalds.

Alasdair MacColl led the Macdonalds of the Keppoch clan —only one hundred of them, because their chief, a Protestant, would not allow them to bring along a priest. There was Kinloch-Moidart, with one hundred more men; stocky, beef-faced Young Clanranald with three hundred men, indifferently armed but eager to fight; the Macdonald of Tiern-

drich and his small band; the MacIan of Glencoe, who led
sixty warriors keen for revenge; the Macdonald of Glengarry,
in a beautiful dress tartan, his men, though, not so comfort-
ably clad.

Then the Camerons came, four abreast, bare knees swinging, eight pipers blowing up with all the strength in their
lungs. The Camerons made a happy display. The Young
Lochiel marched at their head: he was in his forties, but
perk, his eyes atwinkle, a smile on his face. Angus Mac-
Clarke, MacMaryin of Letterfinlay, Taylor of Cowal, and
faithful Bobbie MacUalrig were just behind him, and behind
them were the ordinary gentlemen, and the helots.

The Camerons made up the largest group of all. After
they had gone there was a break in the procession. Then the
Glenallans came. And Lady Helen leaned forward so far that
she all but fell out of the window.

Gerald cried, astounded: "Damn me, if that isn't the young
barbarian who was afraid to fight Fitzstephen! He's mighty
cocky now, ain't he?"

There was, indeed, no man there prouder than Sir Malcolm MacIldowie of Glenallan. He had insisted that his clan
be placed a telling distance behind the Camerons. It infuriated him to have people think that his men owed allegiance
to the Young Lochiel, that he himself was only a chieftain,
head of a sept. Then, too, with all the Cameron pipers blowing, the strains that Old Angus was able to produce from
Old Angus's father's set of pipes would scarcely be heard if
the clans were close together. It must not be thought that
Old Angus was piping the "Black Donald March." He was,
instead, giving the *Spaidsearachd Ailien Oig*, or, "The March
of Young Allan," and he was giving it with all the energy left
in his lungs.

Malcolm for this occasion had donned his dress tartan, brilliant red and yellow, which swung at his knees and billowed

behind him. Evan of Lochallan walked on his right, followed by his gillie, and on the left was the phlegmatic Walter MacPhail. Behind the chief went Gillie Angus with the musket; and behind him were the three sons of MacMichael Roy, and vacant-faced Dafty. Old Angus, of course, was in the fore, the place for a piper.

"Mighty cocky," Gerald repeated. "You'd think Glenallan had the whole kingdom behind him, the way he walks."

"He's handsome," Lady Helen said simply. "He was never like that in London. Look at the strides he takes."

Gerald shrugged.

"Oh, he's a nine days' wonder—"

The Glenallans were followed by the Stuarts of Appine, under quiet Ardshiel, two hundred of them, trim warriors. Then came Cluny Macpherson of Cluny, and his son, the Young Macpherson of Breaknachie, with one hundred and fifty clansmen, all in their brave red tartan. And then there were one hundred of the Grants of Glenmoriston.

"That's our clan, Gerald!"

"Since when have you turned Scotch?"

"Your grandmother was a Grant," Robert Forbes reminded him.

"That don't make *me* a yapping savage, does it?"

There was another break in the procession. The clans had all marched past. The Lowland regiments were gone. There remained only the prince, and the prince came at the end because he knew the value of a theatrical effect. From the windows of Robert Forbes' house they could hear the cheering, approaching in waves, as the crowd caught sight of him. It would seem that everybody in Edinburgh—and why not? —was yelling at the top of his lungs. The noise was so great that it even drowned the music of the pipes.

"For which thank God," Gerald muttered.

Yet even Gerald could not help but whistle in admiration when Charles Edward Stuart rode by.

An exceptionally fine horseman on an exceptionally fine horse—a bay gelding that stepped as though it realized it was carrying a prince of the blood royal—Charles Edward was tall and slender and incredibly graceful. He smiled, and waved his hand. He wore a blue velvet bonnet bound with gold lace and topped with a white rose; a short tartan coat; a blue sash trimmed with gold lace; red velvet smallclothes; black military boots. At his side hung a silver-hilted claymore. On his breast glittered the Star of St. Andrew.

He looked like a figure from a fairy tale. He looked like a maiden's vision come to life. You scarcely dared to breathe for fear that your breath would break a charm and cause him to vanish. You scarcely dared to blink lest he disappear.

Gerald Hornsby grabbed his sister's wrists.

"Stop throwing kisses, you fool!"

But she pushed him away, never taking her eyes from the prince.

The prince rode slowly, one hand on the hilt of the sword, one hand saluting. He smiled right and left, and occasionally, inspired by a shouted witticism, he laughed aloud. He passed Robert Forbes' house, waving gaily. . . .

Lady Helen called for her cape.

"I'm going down to the Cross. No, don't try to stop me, Gerald!"

"At least let me go with you. It's not safe in this crowd."

"Come along then."

The prince entered Holyroodhouse, where of yore his ancestors had dwelt—ancient Holyrood, where the Stuarts had been married and had danced and had played, where the walls were pregnant with memory and the halls hummed with the music of the past. The multitude was quiet as the prince passed those portals. He himself was quiet.

Then the proclamation was read at the Cross. Mr. Secretary Murray did the reading, and in a clear hard voice. Around the Cross were the improvised cavalry, in trews and philabegs. Outside of the circle these fellows formed with their horses were the clansmen, waving their bonnets and shouting in Gaelic. Murray of Broughton's wife, an Amazon astride a magnificent stallion, distributed white cockades to the faithful Jacobites and the newly-converted.

Lady Helen looked in vain for the Glenallan. And not finding him, she joined her voice with the others in calling for the prince to appear again.

He consented, stepping out on a balcony where all of them could see him. The roar was deafening. The prince waved his hand, and smiled to right and left.

"Damn you, stop cheering for him," Gerald whispered.

"I won't," cried Lady Helen. "He's the most gallant man I've ever seen, and I'm going to cheer all I want!"

"He's *good looking*. But I don't see what that has to do with it."

"He's *gallant*, Gerald! Look—he came here all alone. No help from France, no help from Spain, no money, practically no friends. Gerald, admit it, that's a courageous thing to do!"

"Well, there are courageous men in Whitefriars.

"You have no *feeling*, Gerald!"

In this way they returned to Robert Forbes' house, jostled and pushed, obliged to shout at each other to make themselves heard.

Lady Helen strongly denied that she was a rebel. But she might be, she granted, after one more look at that young man on the balcony. *He,* she explained, was the sort of man who should be a king, whether by divine right or by parliamentary sanction or in any other manner. A king should be a king, not a drunken little German beast.

"When they have you locked in a dungeon, you won't feel so fine about it," Gerald grumbled.

Their host himself met them at the door. Robert Forbes was a quiet, easygoing man, not given to excitement; but there was a tremble in his voice when he informed Lady Helen that she had a visitor, come during her trip to the Cross.

"A young Highlander, no less. An arrogant laddie, too. Just bristles with feathers and pistols. Really, I was afraid of him—at first."

CHAPTER 7

THE CHANGE IN Malcolm that Lady Helen had remarked when Malcolm was on parade was even more apparent now that he was in the same room with her. He seemed infinitely strong, ready at a signal to grab the world with one hand and toss it into some undiscoverable corner of the cosmos.

Lady Helen had remembered him as a shy, cautious young man, uneasy in his English clothes, giving the impression that he was too tightly bound, too closely confined, for comfort. But now his feet were spread, his hands were on his hips, and there was a light of suppressed excitement in his eyes.

"You asked me to call on my way back to London."

"It is good to see you again."

Gerald, hovering in the dorway, was silent. Robert Forbes, too, who was with Gerald, said never a word this while. Lady Helen beckoned them both.

"Gerald, you and Mr. Glenallan have already met. . . . Robert, this is Mr. Malcolm Glenallan, the son of the Laird of Glenallan. Mr. Robert Forbes, sir, my cousin."

Malcolm nodded. Robert Forbes started to bow, but paused

halfway when he saw the coolness with which he was greeted. As for Gerald, he was still scowling.

There was an awkward pause. Lady Helen remembered that there were always awkward pauses when the Young Glenallan was a member of the party.

"Your men have been most fortunate," Robert Forbes ventured at last.

"Aye."

Forbes took snuff, closed the box, tapped it, offered it to Malcolm.

"A pinch from my mill, sir?"

These two were Scots, even though one came from Lochaber, the other Edinburgh; and Robert Forbes was not at all a belligerent sort of man.

"Thank you." The Glenallan took snuff. "I hope my presence doesn't frighten you," he said afterward, a breath of sarcasm in his voice. "His Royal Highness has issued orders against all manner of plundering. You may be sure that nothing of the sort will happen, and doubly sure that I wouldn't be a party to it if it did."

Robert Forbes lied pleasantly.

"I had never expected such a thing, sir." He bowed, backing out of the room. "I shall ask Mrs. Forbes to join you?"

"Please do," said Lady Helen.

"I'll wait for her to come," Gerald announced.

Now the Glenallan was frowning.

"I would rather be alone with Lady Helen," he said.

"I'm not sure that it would be proper for you to be alone with her," Gerald said, very stiff.

"Now, Gerald—"

"Are you going to blame me too, sister? Have you turned rebel entirely?" He banged a fist on the little table. "What's back of this?"

"Nothing is back of it," said Lady Helen. "Mr. Glenallan

has come to visit me, and you've been behaving like a vulgar barrister, that's all. Why don't you get out?"

A thundercloud, Gerald left without having bowed.

"You must forgive my brother, Mr. Glenallan."

"He saved my life once," Malcolm said.

She begged him to be seated. She was graciousness personified, and very lovely in blue and gold, with her own brown hair bound loosely at the back of her small head. She was intensely curious and asked him many questions about Charles Edward Stuart.

"The prince," Malcolm assured her, "is as amiable as he is handsome."

"Do you think he'll appear in public again while he is here?"

"I know he will. He has to raise funds, ye ken. And he plans to give a reception at Holyrood soon. May I escort you?"

The invitation was so abrupt that Lady Helen gasped. She could not reconcile this bold young fellow with the bashful gentleman she had known in London. She stammered acceptance and some manner of thanks. Gerald would be furious, of course, but she could trouble about that afterward.

It was at this point that Mrs. Forbes entered the room, a delayed duenna. To her and to Helen, after many questions, the young laird explained his costume—what it meant, why it was so arranged and so colored, how it was used.

"This is my dress tartan, this design on the plaid. My brother and myself are the only persons privileged to wear it, now that my father is dead. Perhaps you noticed that my men wore a dark tartan? That's the war tartan. I can wear that too, if I wish, and I do when I'm hunting. . . . This? Why, this is my sporran. It's a purse, see? It opens at the top. . . . On the brooch? Why, the MacIldowie arms. Oh, yes, we have escutcheons too."

His target fascinated the ladies. There was something irresistibly romantic, in an age of gunpowder and copybook armies, to find a real soldier, an officer in a genuine revolution, equipped with a shield. And aside from this, the target was a beautiful piece. It was perfectly round. The outside was covered with tightly stretched leather tooled in a foliaceous design, with an enormous brass boss in the center, four smaller bosses surrounding this, and many little brass studs and nails, all brilliantly polished, arranged geometrically upon its surface. The back was covered with calfskin and padding. There were two armholes and a fist grip. In addition, in the back of the target there was a sheath for a triangular dirk. There was no handle but a screw-end to this dirk, which before battle, could be affixed to the big central boss so that it stuck out like a unicorn's horn. Malcolm so affixed it for their edification, smiling at the breathless interest they displayed.

Lady Helen, however, was most attracted by the dress tartan, a red mixture not unlike that of the Glengarry Macdonalds. She thought it the most beautiful pattern she had ever seen. How in the world was it made?

"Bitter vetch and pivet berries, when they're ripe, with salt, and a little water flag and bog myrtle."

"Oh."

"I have some extra dress breacan with me," the Glenallan said. "If you like, I'll send you some this afternoon."

Mrs. Forbes indicated disapproval, but Malcolm was paying scant attention to Mrs. Forbes. Lady Helen herself wanted to accept the gift, but she was doubtful of the propriety of acceptance.

"It is very kind of you, sir, but if only you and your brother can wear it—"

"I am the chief of the clan," Malcolm said. "I alone can give you permission to wear it. And I do."

"Oh—"

Now Mrs. Forbes was suspicious.

"And what does that mean?" she asked.

"It means," Malcolm explained, "that the lady is accepted by me as a member of my clan. The clansmen are at her service whenever she would call them, unless I instruct them otherwise. None of them will ever do her any harm or fail to avenge any harm that is done to her. It means that she will always have hospitality in Glenallan."

"That is a lot for a piece of cloth to mean," the dubious Mrs. Forbes suggested.

"It is Glenallan cloth," Malcolm pointed out. He turned to Lady Helen. "I'll send it by a gillie who speaks some English, if you should want to ask him any questions."

Yes, this was a different man. Those little unconscious rudenesses, which in London had seemed to mar his character, fitted perfectly with the rough grandeur of the kilt. His arrogance, never displayed directly to Lady Helen but apparent in every other act of his, was of a piece with the eagle feathers, the claymore, the pistols. His long legs and thick muscular arms at last had a chance to expand, to stretch and swell in primitive exuberance as the Glenallan moved.

He asked and was granted permission to call the following day. He had appeared to expect that this would be granted him. Indeed, refusal of anything would have amazed this feudal baron, a tyrant at twenty-four. He bowed gravely and quit the house, and Lady Helen and Mrs. Forbes watched him from the window as he swung with long strides down the street, contemptuously disregarding the stares of the citizens.

The plaid arrived an hour later. It was some eight feet long and half as wide, very pleasant to the touch. Gillie Angus brought it. He was quiet, careful. He assured Lady Helen that the wearing of this cloth anywhere in Lochaber would be a protection against all human danger so long as the houses of Lochiel and Glenallan were in power.

"An' they always will be," Gillie Angus promised her solemnly.

After he had gone, Lady Helen spent the sort of evening which, a few hours previous, would have seemed to her intolerably dull. She did not visit, or even play cards. She devoted herself instead to mere thinking—thinking about the young chief and the striking figure he made and the strength he had shown. She thought still longer, perhaps, about the way in which he had gazed at her all during the visit. Lady Helen was sufficiently accustomed to flattery, of which there was an abundance in London. But there was about this young man a determined admiration, a blunt and indubitably honest desire.

She had not realized this while he was in her presence. But now that he was gone she marveled that he had not picked her up in his arms and walked away with her—taken her to some distant hillside where the strange Highlandmen lived in ancient, rugged magnificence. Among the fops of London, among the laces and the frills of court, habitually she felt strong. It was a new sensation for her to be a weakling in the presence of a man. Yet—she wouldn't have resisted.

The next afternoon Malcolm called again. As on the previous day, Mrs. Forbes stood guard over them. Lady Helen was not abducted. But the young chief had lost none of his vitality and none of his arrogance. Robert Forbes himself candidly admitted that he was genuinely afraid of the fellow.

"Lord, what a temper he must have," Robert Forbes observed afterward. "I have made inquiries about him. He appears to be a very important personage, in spite of the smallness of his following. His family name is MacIldowie. They are a branch of the Camerons, I believe. But the Highlanders always call him Glenallan, *the* Glenallan, which is the name of his estate, and his own clansmen call him Macdomhnull Dhu, or 'Son of Donald the Black,' which really means *descendant* of Donald the Black. His father was Sir Douglas Glenallan, a famous old trouble-maker. And this young man himself, from what I hear, has been knighted by the Pretender. But I don't think," added the cautious Robert Forbes, "that it would be quite proper for *us* to acknowledge it and call him Sir Malcolm."

"Not yet, anyway," offered Lady Helen.

Malcolm's third visit to the Forbes house was brief.

"We're marching out," he told them. "Cope is coming down and we're going to stop him. May I see you when I return?"

And, when this boon had been granted, he kissed Helen's hand gravely, awarded Mrs. Forbes a formal bow, nodded coolly to Robert Forbes and to Gerald, and departed. His men were waiting for him in the street. He placed himself at their head, with Evan of Lochallan on the right side, Walter MacPhail on the left, the piper in front, and Gillie Angus in the rear with the musket, while behind Gillie Angus were the three sons of MacMichael Roy, and Dafty. He nodded to Old Angus, and the marching song was started.

And thus, with everything in its proper place, Malcolm went off to battle.

CHAPTER 8

CHARLES EDWARD STUART drew his sword and unstrapped and threw away from him the belt and scabbard.

"My friends," he cried, "this day our cause will triumph! We will return with victory or we will not return at all. See, here is my sword—I have thrown away the scabbard!"

They cheered him loudly.

Then they marched out of Duddingstone. A careful gillie, attached to the Duke of Perth, first took the precaution to pick up his highness's sword belt and scabbard.

"He'll thank me later," the gillie explained.

They left Figgat Burn behind them and took the pleasant way through Easter Dunningstone to Musselburgh.

The men were gay. The pipes were playing bravely, and some of the men sang.

> "Oh, who'd na ficht for Charlie?
> "Oh, who'd na draw the sword—"

They went up Edge-buckling Brae, passed around Wallyford and over Fawside Hill, took the post road at Douphiston, ascended Birsley Brae, and, about half a mile west of Tranent, came suddenly upon the enemy.

The men raised a great shout, and would have rushed in immediately had it not been for the efforts of the gentlemen.

The fact is, though they were on higher ground and could start the battle or avoid it, as they pleased, the slope that stretched down between them and the Saxons was marshy and intersected with enclosures, and cut at the bottom by a broad deep ditch alongside of which ran a thick hedge. And so, at length it was decided to camp upon the spot, where at least they were secure from attack, and wait for the morning.

The night was chilly. The day had been clear, but now the skies were overcast and a mist rolled in from the sea and there was a faint drizzle of rain. The Englishmen below had lighted great campfires, which glared through the darkness, round and yellow and geometrically spaced.

The Glenallans were not given sentry duty, and soon after the final arrangements for the day had been made, they wrapped themselves in their plaids and went to sleep.

Malcolm was awakened by Donald of Lochiel, who shook

his shoulder and whispered to him. It was utterly dark. The drizzle had ceased, but the mist was thick about them.

"Sh-sh! No questions now! Come along!"

He led Malcolm to a field of cut peas, where his royal highness, wrapped in a tartan blanket, was seated on a pile of straw. Evidently, he too had just been awakened. Nearby were the high officers of the army. Before the prince stood Robert Anderson, an East Lothian gentleman, son of Anderson of Whitburgh.

Young Lochiel whispered to his cousin:

"He says he knows a path by which we can go around the swamp and get between the Saxons and the sea without being exposed. It's high ground there, too, he says, and all dry."

Anderson swore again that if he were made guide for the army this night he could lead all the men to the other side in safety. He had hunted over this ground many times, he said. His talk was convincing. It was decided to start the march immediately. The men were awakened. They adjusted their plaids and fell into line, two columns of three abreast. They marched in the deepest silence, careful not to let their weapons click.

The prince was wildly exuberant, like a boy at his first fair. When they came to the ditch at the foot of the hill, he cried, "See if I can jump it!" and made a mighty attempt to do so, falling short, however, by a few inches, and thereby covering himself with mud. He laughed, forgetting the need for silence. Immediately there came an English voice:

"Who goes there?"

The Highlanders gave no answer, but stood still. Three shots were heard, then the receding sound of hoofbeats on the soft wet earth. A wee ribbon of smoke, in which there was the smell of gunpowder, drifted past their faces.

"Dragoons," said Mr. Secretary Murray.

But the prince only laughed again.

"It doesn't matter. Mr. Anderson tells me that we have already come far enough to be safe. Does any other man think he can make that jump?"

Nobody volunteered. Malcolm believed he could do it, but for that very reason he did not try, fearing to embarrass Prince Charles; so he hitched up his kilt and waded across, as the others were doing.

Then for a time they were on an upgrade. The way was rough, but the morass was behind them now and the agile Highlanders had no difficulty with rocks. It was dawn, but the mist obscured the enemy.

Finally they halted, having, according to Anderson, reached a spot exactly opposite to the position they had previously been holding.

"Keep the men awake," was the order; but the men in fact were much too excited even to think of sleep.

The charge was to be made as soon as the clans had been wheeled into position. The Macdonalds were given their usual post of honor on the right wing. In the center were the Macgregors and the Duke of Perth's men. The left consisted of the Camerons, the Glenallans, and the Athole regiment, Stewarts. Prince Charles commanded the second line, only fifty yards in the rear.

Malcolm, facing his clansmen, raised his right hand for attention.

"On your knees, laddies."

They obeyed, uncovering.

"Almighty God, preserve bravery. Preserve our prince and make his arms victorious this day. Give each man courage and strength, for Thou knowest there are no men who worship Thee more truly. In the name of the Father, and of the Son, and of the Holy Ghost—amen."

"Amen," the Glenallans echoed, and rose to their feet.

Now all along the line targets were unslung, poniards were unsheathed, and plaids were tightened or cast off. Malcolm wrapped his own plaid firmly under the broad leather belt, screwed a dirk into the boss of his shield, pulled his bonnet far down on his head, took his musket from the hands of Gillie Angus, made certain that his claymore was loose in its scabbard.

"Scrug your bonnets, laddies!"

The command to advance came, and they started forward at a rapid walk, their feet whispering through the stubble.

It was hard to walk, and they soon broke into a trot. Then a breeze came from the sea at their backs, blowing the mist away, and those in the front line saw the enemy.

In spite of himself, Malcolm felt his heart sink. General Cope had, indeed, been warned of the Highlanders' movement, and he was ready for their attack. There were artillery and cavalry at each wing, and a solid line of infantry between. The red coats and high, pointed hats were clear through what mist was left; and from a thousand places on muskets and cannon and sabers came gleams of light. The precision was frightful. Malcolm looked to right and left, remarking the contrast that Charlie's men made. They were ragged, barefoot, ignorant. They advanced obliquely because the command to charge had reached the left wing first. Scarcely two hundred muskets or fowling pieces were to be seen among them, the rest of the weapons being claymores, scythe blades, and Lochaber axes, though a few men even carried studded clubs, while some of the Macgregors relied on long bows. There were no bayonets, no cannon.

Malcolm cursed himself. Was this fear? He glanced at his men to see whether they had observed any change of expression that his face might have displayed for an instant. But they were intent upon the foe. Old Angus alone was looking back, awaiting an order. Malcolm nodded.

"Blow up."

He raised his musket and fired. He threw the musket to the ground, drew his claymore and raised it. With the opening notes of the bagpipes came his battle cry.

"Glenallan! Glenallan!"

The men broke into a full run—a sprint. They, too, shrieked the battle cry.

"Glenallan!"

The infantry fired one volley at them, and the smoke blew back into Saxon faces. Malcolm, whose long legs had carried him ahead of the others, burst through this smoke and came upon a company of dragoons. He had been advised to strike at the horses' noses when he met cavalry. But he had no chance to do this. The dragoons discharged their carbines and wheeled and dashed away. The very sight of the Wild Scots charging downhill had been too much for them.

Malcolm fired a pistol after them and immediately ran to his right, where there was a company of foot soldiers desperately reloading. One of them stepped out of line to meet him. Malcolm caught the bayonet on his target, dropping to his left knee to do so; and he turned off the point and struck a full blow on the head. The soldier dropped.

The other foot soldiers, seemingly frightened by somebody behind Malcolm, turned and ran away.

A dragoon, whose horse had gone wild under him and was beyond control, came stamping among the clansmen. They dodged quickly. Dafty's long Lochaber ax, hook-ended, caught the fellow's coat and pulled him to the ground; and at the same instant Gillie Angus leaped underneath the animal, and slit open its belly with a poniard. In springing aside, Malcolm had slipped on the wet ground and fallen to his knees. He rose in time to see Dafty cut the fallen dragoon's throat. He grabbed the half-wit, shook him fiercely.

"If I catch you doing that again, I'll knife you myself!"

Dafty nodded. He could not understand the reason for this instruction, but the instruction itself was clear.

An old man, evidently a major or colonel of the dragoons, came running up from the rear, trying to rally whatever foot soldiers would stand with him, since his own men had run. Some fifty or sixty redcoats supported him. But the Camerons were nearest this group, and reached it first, and by the time the Glenallans got to it there was little left to do but loot. Malcolm had no stomach for slaughter. Great Davie, with his terrible sword, and Walter MacPhail, bellowing at the top of his lungs, could not be restrained: they hurled themselves into the killing and did not stop until the redcoats had thrown down their muskets and called for quarter.

It was astounding. All of this had occupied barely five minutes. The Highlanders had scarcely begun to fight, and there were some even in the first line who had not struck a blow; yet the battle was over.

The Highlanders ran everywhere, stripping the bodies of dead and wounded alike, taking coats and muskets and watches and wigs. The wigs were a delightful novelty. All of Cope's baggage, including his military chest, had fallen into the hands of Prince Charlie's men, and there were many wigs in the baggage, for Cope's officers must go to war properly provided. Half the Macdonald helots and all of the Macgregors were fitted out with powdered perukes, and they danced around screaming at one another and making faces. One man was vastly excited to find himself in possession of a mirror: he had never before seen a mirror. Another had a watch which he was trying to feed, assuming from the noise it made that it was some kind of animal.

The Camerons, on the whole, were well behaved, and the Glenallans, being so few, were easily controlled. But the helots of the Great Clan Colla, and the Robertsons, and

Maclaughlins, and Grants, and Macgregors ran wild, taking everything they could find.

The field was hideously bloody. There were English soldiers who had literally been hacked to pieces—headless, armless, legless. Great Davie, according to Walter MacPhail, who had witnessed it, had cut one man exactly in half at the waist with a blow behind which Davie had put all his strength. It was said that a Clanranald had, with a down blow, crushed a skull completely and sunk his blade as far as the chin. Malcolm stepped over one poor devil who had been laid open from the right armpit almost to the hip bone. The corpses were the more terrible because they had been stripped. The white of bare skin, and the red of blood, almost blotted the brown earth from sight.

Malcolm came to some men who were carrying Evan Macgregor from the field. Evan had been wounded twice and was unable to walk, but his eyes were sparkling. He grinned at Malcolm.

"I'll bring that bottle of brandy to your quarters tonight," Malcolm promised.

Macgregor held out a whisky flask.

"A drink on it now, Callum. It's been worthy of our fathers!"

Malcolm smiled and took the flask.

"*Deoch slaint an Righ,*" he murmured, and drank.

CHAPTER 9

AFTER THE CELEBRATION WAS finished and the shouting had died, the Glenallan renewed his visits to Robert Forbes' house in the Cannongate.

"It was no battle," he told them. "There could not be a battle when the Saxons didn't fight."

He was true to his promise about Holyroodhouse. His invitation to Lady Helen was made definite. Cope disposed of, Prince Charles entertained; and Malcolm and Helen attended. She met the prince. More, she danced three times with him.

The army was encamped outside the city, but the military council met every day at the palace and discussed plans. Prince Charles was in favor of marching directly into England, convinced as he was that they would be re-enforced there by Jacobites.

"London is our next prize! We have taken one capital—we must take the other!"

The chiefs were not optimistic. Scotland was theirs, true, but there remained a great deal of Hanoverian feeling; and in spite of the ovation the prince was given whenever he appeared in public, the majority of the Lowlanders probably were foolish enough still to favor the German's rule, though not zealous enough to fight for it. The mass of the English regular troops had not yet been brought into the field. Then, too, there was the castle. Could it be said that an army possessed Scotland when Edinburgh Castle was in enemy hands?

Promptly after their entrance into the city, the Highlanders had formed a blockade, and when Cope had been defeated, leaving no prospect of immediate relief for the castle garrison, it seemed certain that General Guest would ask for terms. General Guest did nothing of the sort. Instead, he sent down word that unless the blockade were lifted he would open his guns upon the city.

Prince Charles was shocked.

"Barbarous!" he cried.

But—the siege was lifted.

For the most part, however, the talk at council sessions was concerned with less interesting features of the campaign. The raising of funds, the conduct of the men, the ordering of provisions and arms. Almost every day the prince promised them that aid would come from France; but the aid did not come.

Meanwhile, they drilled and equipped themselves. The original force had made little pretense at military organization, marching in whatever order seemed most convenient at the hour; but in Edinburgh there was a considerable change in the arrangement of the clans.

Mr. Secretary Murray and the Young Lochiel and Lord George, also the prince himself, were busy forming regiments. It was Sir Thomas Sheridan who proposed that the Glenallans be joined with the Gordons, giving as his reason the fact that the Camerons, with whom the Glenallans logically belonged, were already more numerous than most of the Highland regiments, whereas the Gordons needed about a dozen men to round out their group.

Malcolm protested, and so did the Young Lochiel. But Sir Thomas was close to his highness, and the order was signed.

The Glenallans, to a man, laid down their arms. They would follow only a descendant of the Black Donald. Not even a Gordon of Glenbucket would satisfy them. If their own chief must be superseded, then they would follow the Young Lochiel, with their own chief in immediate command. Otherwise they would go home. No amount of argument could dissuade them, and eventually the order was rescinded; the clan remained a sort of independent company under the captaincy of Malcolm, who, however, accepted commands only from the Stuart himself.

All of this Lady Helen learned at Robert Forbes' house in the Cannongate. Her visitor was becoming more loquacious these days. With proper urging, and a carefully kept silence when silence was demanded, he could be induced to tell her many things about the army and about himself and his clan.

Once she ventured to ask him about the affair at Martin's. The Glenallan's face darkened.

"How did you learn that?"

"Captain Fitzstephen himself told me. I met him the next morning on the Mall."

He said nothing, but it was plain that he was angry, and she was sorry she had spoken. Nevertheless, she was intensely curious about this episode, and she put another question.

"Was it because you were coming here that you did not want a duel?"

"Aye."

"And was that why you advised me not to come here, that night? Because you knew there would be war?"

"Aye."

"Are you sorry I came?"

He seemed startled, then puzzled. He looked up quickly, studying her as though he suspected her of making sport of him.

"Sorry? Why, I'm in love with you!"

Now Lady Helen Hornsby had been told often enough, and in many different ways, sometimes very eloquently, that she was beloved. And the declaration never failed to thrill her, for she was, after all, a woman. But this young Highlander's frank, almost impolite statement left her without speech.

Malcolm's honesty was almost too much. She was not accustomed to sincerity. In the presence of an emotion so intense she felt like a baby. She nodded weakly, not even rising, when he excused himself.

Why, I'm in love with you!

If any other man but Malcolm Glenallan had said that she would have laughed. She didn't laugh at him. She couldn't.

That night he called again. He was to take her to Holyrood, where Prince Charles was giving another reception.

He made no reference to the episode of the afternoon, but walked beside her chair and chatted pleasantly on the way to the ball. In the ballroom itself she saw little of him. He did not care for the sliding, unacrobatic, Lowland dances; and he believed that he was depriving her of pleasure when he intruded his presence upon her at such a function. He spent most of his time that night in conversation with other Highland gentlemen. He was not unlike a father who escorts his pretty daughter to a ball and smiles at her innocent pleasures there but keeps his own mind occupied with important, parental matters.

The trip home was more eventful. It was a clear night, not cold, with the sky very close to the earth. Again Malcolm walked by the side of her chair, Gillie Angus trailing them at a discreet distance. Malcolm was quiet. He frowned at the paving stones.

Helen did not speak. She was embarrassed, the memory of Malcolm's declaration hot within her.

"Soon we're going out of the city," he said at last.

She offered timidly that it might be better for him to keep military plans to himself.

"It's no secret," he cried. "Charlie's bent on going to London. He thinks Englishmen will join us along the way. I —I don't like it." He scowled at the pavement. "But Charlie will get his way. He's stubborn as a bull. He says we're not recruiting any more men here and we might as well start south now, before the German gets his full army back from Flanders."

"Well, Gerald and I will be leaving soon too, I believe. It —it's been pleasant here. Balls at the palace and everything. . . . It doesn't seem possible there is a civil war going on, does it? You know, I like Edinburgh. I didn't at first, but I do now."

"Aye. It's better than London."

At Robert Forbes' house, after the carriers and link boys had been dismissed, he grabbed her arm.

"Eilidh—"

Her thin brown eyebrows wrinkled together; her face was a question mark.

The Glenallan shook an impatient head.

"That's Gaelic. It means Helen—"

His hand on her arm hurt her, but she was afraid to move.

"This afternoon you jumped when I told you I love you. Hadn't you known that?"

She shook her head.

"No. No, I—I hadn't known."

He released her. Fisting her hips, he frowned at her.

"Of course I love you! How can I help loving you, and you as beautiful and sweet as you are? I loved you when I first met you, and I love you more now, and more every day!"

He showed as though about to seize her again; but he stopped suddenly, dropped his arms to his sides, and made a bow. He apologized for his behavior. He was ashamed of himself, he said, because he could not control his feelings. Would Lady Helen forgive him?

She scrutinized him, anxious, worried. She feared that he was angry; yet his anger seemed rather to be directed inwardly against himself than outwardly against her. He bowed again. And they parted in silence.

But the next day, when Malcolm came to Robert Forbes' house, he called her Eilidh.

There was a relentlessness about this courtship that frightened her. Malcolm kept after her as a hunter might pursue a wounded deer. Yet, always he was honest. His code was full and firm, a genuine part of himself. If prisoner she must be, Lady Helen reflected, she could not hope for a more reliable turnkey.

Charles Edward Stuart knelt as in prayer, in the drafty little chapel at Holyrood. He was not praying; he was thinking; but it looked well to kneel there in silence, alone, while the early morning sunbeams oozed through stained-glass windows and the wee red light at the altar flickered nervously. And he needed to look well. There were men watching him from the doorway, and they would report this prayer to other men, and would relate how devout was the bonnie young prince. He needed that, aye. More and more, as this business progressed, he was coming to know how much his personal appearance counted. It was incredible that these harsh mountaineers should even think of his looks: it was his blood, his breeding, rather than his countenance, that they should consider. But he knew, now, that there were many in the ranks who were out to fight, and possibly to die, largely because Charles Edward Stuart was picturesque, graceful, gracious, a figure out of old chivalry. He rather despised them for this; but if they were willing to serve he was in no position to cavil about their inspiration. So he knelt in prayer, while the men in the doorway watched.

Within an hour they would start south. The real war was yet to come. Louis of France had not responded. The Lowlanders were lukewarm. Charles pretended to believe that the people of Lancaster, at least, would rise to a man and flock toward his banner; and a few weeks earlier he had truly believed this; but he was having doubts. Upon the Highlanders, that ragged band of ruffians, everything appeared to depend. And he could not understand the Highlanders. He could not get a grip on them. They obeyed him when they pleased; but when they differed from him they said so, emphatically. Scotland they were willing to conquer. But England was another place.

But he had won the prolonged argument in council. They

were marching into England. As soon as he rose, they would start.

Charles was not frightened. There was too much to do ever to think of fear. Nevertheless, doubts were swarming about him like gnats at night, millions of them, giving him no rest. He wished to be rid of doubts, if only for this brief kneeling period in the chapel. He wished to rest a little, to think of nothing at all, while he seemed to be praying—just to press his hands over his hot eyes and push away all thoughts and doubts and dreams, leaving his mind a refreshed, clean thing. But it was impossible.

He heard the men in the doorway shuffle. He had been here, he estimated, long enough. The impression had been made.

He wished, as he rose to his feet, that he had really been able to pray. Sometimes he could do so; but only at night, and when he was lying down—never when anybody watched him.

He caught himself exhaling the tiniest sigh, and he stifled this. It was with a properly serious face that he left the chapel.

Mr. Secretary Murray, wearing a characteristic frown, and clutching a handful of papers, was waiting for him. Charles spoke first.

"Is the baggage ready? Have the cavalry been posted? I want a display of whatever cavalry we have."

"They will be ready soon, Highness. Elphinstone is to report to you here."

"Perhaps it would be well if I showed myself once again—" He started for a balcony.

"There is one more matter, Highness. You've promised—"

"What is that? Oh, yes! Our Glenallan would enter the married state. Is he here?"

Malcolm strode in. He was in full war regalia, carrying all

his weapons except the musket, which Gillie Angus toted in the rear. Three eagle feathers were stuck into his bonnet. His plaid was fresh, unwrinkled. The butts of his pistols glittered.

"Your Highness is kind to stand with me."

"I'm delighted to have the opportunity. It is gratifying to know that the MacIldowie line will persist, and especial cause for rejoicing to know that the chief of this honorable clan is to take so lovely a bride. She is here?"

"She is in the next room, Highness."

"Summon her, and we'll start. It, uh, it's an odd time for marrying, Glenallan."

"I am aware of that, Sire."

"Surely you know you'll be obliged to leave your wife right away. I'd be delighted if I was able to give you leave to remain behind for a few days, but you yourself know that we can't spare a single man, much less so valuable an officer as you."

"Aye," said Malcolm.

Lady Helen came on Robert Forbes' arm. She wore simple brown and gold, and her hair was not powdered. A fringed Spanish glove was on her right hand, but her left hand was bare to receive the ring. She was demure in manner, as befits a bride, keeping her gaze on the floor even while she curtsied.

The prince raised her.

"Maidens have gone to the marriage altar in greater state," he said, "but I think one never went there with such sincere admiration of all who saw her. When my royal father and I are at St. James's Palace in London, I will command you to appear before us in this same gown you wear now."

Highlanders were thick about them. All cousins, no doubt. Glenallan, the prince reflected, appeared to be related to almost every important family in the north. Strange people.

. . . He wondered if he would ever be able to get their complicated genealogies straight in his mind. Meanwhile, it would be a good time for some repeatable compliment, something they'd remember.

"I think," he said, rather louder than before, "that any woman in this world could well be pleased to enter such a distinguished family as that of MacIldowie, whose members have always been among my royal father's staunchest friends and most beloved subjects."

There was a mutter of approval. Yes, these men were cousins.

"Shall we go inside, gentlemen? Time presses."

It was a Catholic chapel, but an Anglican minister had been persuaded to perform the ceremony. This was highly irregular. Gerald Hornsby, who had refused even to attend, had sworn that it would be no legal marriage at all; and many of the gentlemen who attended were whispering that it was no marriage anyway, by Scottish law, until it had been consummated. And there was a very excellent chance, they pointed out to one another, that it never would. Sir Malcolm might not come back from England.

But Helen had agreed to it. She wanted it. Malcolm would be her husband, even if she never saw him again. She tried not to think about this. Surrounded by strange, barbarically attired mountaineers, who spoke a tongue unknown to her, herself attended only by her cousins the Forbes, Helen dared not even lift her head until she found herself at the altar next to Malcolm. He did not touch her, and she did not glance at him; but just to feel his presence, to know that he was close to her, was enough.

It was almost brutally brief. Afterward they marched out together, side by side, the ring burning on her finger, her glance again upon the stones of the floor. She was able to murmur the polite things while her hand was being kissed, and to smile and smile. . . . Malcolm stood beside her, straight and serious. The men kissed her hand, said things, and backed away, for they were still in the presence of the Stuart, upon whom one must not turn one's back. Soon Charles Edward himself embraced her, tenderly, informally, and he too departed. There was much to be done outside. The army was ready to move, and the pipes were being played. Men hurried off. Sir Malcolm and Lady Glenallan were left alone in the bleak brown corridor.

He kissed her quietly, firmly, holding her tight.

"I must go too. Don't be afraid."

"You'll come back! You must come back!"

"Sh-sh. It's a war that will be over soon. We'll be together and happy—or we'll be finished. But whatever it is, we'll know about it soon."

Somebody around a corner coughed, apologetically.

"Macdomhnull Dhu—"

"I'm coming," said Malcolm.

He kissed her again. He started to say something, but he was not able to say it. He held her tight and shook his head, smiled a fleet smile and kissed her once again. Then he released her and walked quickly around the corner of the corridor and away, never looking back. Within half an hour, never having glimpsed her again, he was out of the city, marching at the head of his clan—marching for the border.

CHAPTER 10

THE HIGHLAND ARMY HAD crossed the border, captured Carlysle, dodged General Wade's superior force, outdistanced the Duke of Cumberland and his enormous command, passed through Manchester, and arrived at Derby, less than seventy-five miles from London, on the fourth of December in the year of our Lord 1745.

Londoners had become panicky. The banks were mobbed; wealthy men and women were taking ship for the continent; the royal yacht had been put into readiness, and the royal jewels and art treasures were packed aboard; men were hiding their valuables in their cellars, and women who subscribed to the general belief that the Wild Scots were cannibals who ate babies were frantically and in many cases successfully endeavoring to persuade their husband to quit the city.

The Highland chiefs knew nothing of this. They only knew that enlistments had been trifling, desertions considerable; that another army was preparing to meet them at London, and that, even if this defensive force were defeated, and the city taken, the Duke of Cumberland, with an army that was double the size of the Highland army, would be down upon them before they could see to the proper fortification of the place.

In Derby, the Glenallan was quartered with Lochallan and Walter MacPhail at Mr. Littlehorse's house. There the Young Lochiel visited him.

"Ye heard of the council that's to be tonight, Callum?"

"Aye."

"Ye ken what it means?"

"Aye. It means that we have been men long enough and now we're going to be cowards."

"Don't be a fool, Callum! The only thing we can do is retreat. Have ye not heard that the German's men have taken Edinburgh again, and the Campbells and the Macleods and the Rosses have been raised against us? Ye ken what they'll do to our own country, Callum? It's the hills we should be protecting! If the Englishmen want their lawful king, let *them* fight for him!"

Malcolm opened a bottle of brandy, drank deep, wiped his mouth, walked to a window. He was too angry to talk.

In the street below, Old Angus was playing a fiddle somebody had found for him, and Paul MacMichael was doing a jig to the vast amusement of ten or twelve towns-people. Across the way was a blacksmith's shop, and there were collected the rest of the Glenallans, together with several Camerons and a few Gordons. They were eager for the taking of London, and had gone to this shop in order to have their claymores sharpened. They were quarreling about precedence, while the smith waited patiently, wonderingly, not daring to start with one weapon until it was determined whose weapon this should be.

Glenbucket's *comhsreang* contended that his inherited position as the gillie who held the rein of a Gordon's horse at dangerous passes entitled him, of course, to go before the helmet carrier of even a descendant of Donald the Black—a contention Great Davie was in no wise prepared to grant.

"You'll vote for retreat?" the Young Lochiel asked anxiously.

"I'll not vote at all," said Malcolm.

Lochiel too took a drink from the bottle, and he banged it down on the table.

"It's a mean business, Callum. I ken that—we all ken it. But damn me, Callum, what else can be done? God be my witness, no man loves Prince Charlie more than I love him and no man is ready to risk more for his cause! But can ye deny it, Callum, that he's more intent upon getting London than upon treating us as we deserve to be treated? Can ye say that our giving up everything we own has made him more respectful of our own rights and our own duties to our gentles and helots? Does he listen to us the way he listens to Kelly? Does he heed Lord George the way he heeds that

damned stiff-neck Sheridan? I tell ye, Callum, we've got to
go back! There's nothing left for us to do!"

Malcolm turned away from the window and took another,
very long pull from the bottle. When he spoke again, his
voice was not so harsh.

"You and I should not quarrel, Donald. You're right and
I'm wrong. But I'll not vote at all in the council, Donald. I'll
not go."

It was, as Lochiel had said, a mean business. Every chief
knew that Prince Charles was concerned first with England
and was using Scotland only as a steppingstone. He had
landed in Lochaber penniless and practically alone, and had
asked for their support. They had given him this; they had
restored him to the throne of his ancestors. But he wanted
more. He wanted England. Even if he got England it would
be the same old story of history all over again. King of England and Scotland? Say rather King of England and of another little place nearby, a place where the people were poor
and ignorant and troublesome, the climate undesirable, a
place where court would be intolerably dull.

Who wanted Scotland, except in an emergency? James VI,
the first man to be monarch of both countries, had felt that
way; and so had each of his successors; and Charles and his
father were no exceptions. Caledonia was to them a royal
backyard. The great titles, the big grants, the glitter and
pomp of court, would remain in London. And the Jacobites
who had been afraid to fight under his banner would flock
around the young prince when he was restored to St. James's,
and tell him tales about how faithful they had been, and
give him money and promises, and get titles and power from
him; while in the Highlands the starving warriors would be
oppressed by laws designed to "civilize" them.

Malcolm had known after his second or third audience
with Charles Edward what would happen if the Stuart line

were reinstated. And he knew, now, in Derby, that the real fighting was yet to come. German George was importing Dutch and Hessian mercenaries now. Pitted against several small Highland clans would be the veterans of many a continental field, men who had been soldiering all their lives. Pitted against the ingenuity and gallantry of Lord George Murray and the Macdonald of Keppoch would be the professional skill of General Wade, the strength of General Hawley, and the furious, pounding brutality of that dog-faced young Duke of Cumberland. The claymore was a beautiful weapon with a long and glorious history, and for hand-to-hand fighting no man could ask for anything better. But muskets and cannon did not permit such fighting. It was an age of gunpowder, and the chivalrous combat of the old days could not survive.

The whole business made Malcolm a trifle sick. To march upon London or to retreat—it made little difference.

At the council that night the prince was petitioned to return to Scotland. Lord George Murray undertook this thankless task.

"His Royal Highness knows that while we have blood in our veins we will battle for the cause that is his. But there are four armies against one army. There are enemy clansmen about to invade our own countries and ravage them. All the bravery in the world, Your Highness knows, can not prevail against this weight of numbers. We have been disappointed. Let's admit it. We expected reinforcements from France, and they have not come. We expected enlistments among the faithful in this country, and the faithful have hidden themselves at our approach.

"We must retreat. In Scotland there is yet some hope. In England, only extermination awaits us. We are gentlemen— His Highness must remember that—and we do not fight for pay, like common soldiers, but for honor and glory. We have no wish to be ground to pieces in an alien country where the women will spit on our corpses and the merchants will gloat over our graves. If die we must, we will die in Scotland!"

The Stuart sprang to his feet, and his palms slapped with an angry sound against the chair arms. His blue eyes flashed.

"*We will never retreat!* I told you that I had come for a crown or a coffin. Did you think I was boasting?"

There was a heavy silence. Lord George Murray still was on his feet, but there was nothing he could say in answer to this. There was nothing anybody could say.

And the prince continued, harshly at first, with bitterness and sarcasm; but then the old charm began to appear, the charm that had caused so many hard-headed chieftains to make fools of themselves. His voice softened; he spread his hands appealingly, reminding the men of the glories of their clans and families—the magnificent courage of the Macdonalds, the quiet steadfastness of the Gordons, the unwavering loyalty of the Camerons, the fire of the men from Athole. He reminded them of Bannockburn and Flodden Field, of the Great Marquis who had led their ancestors at Kilsyth, of Bonnie Dundee who was called *Ian Dhu nan Cath,* "Black John of the Battles," of Calum More. . . .

He stepped down from the dais and walked among them, tears in his eyes, tears on his smooth round cheeks. He appealed to each of the principal chiefs individually, putting his hands on their shoulders.

"Do not think of me as a prince of the blood royal! Act as you would act if a simple gentleman, a cousin, Charles Edward Stuart, came to you and asked you for help. . . ."

It was difficult; but they listened in silence. They had steeled their souls.

"It would be folly to turn back anyway. What of Cumberland, and what of Wade? We escaped them once. But they've learned our tricks. Can we expect to escape them again? You, my Lord Murray, have had the temerity to suggest that my cause already is lost and my arms already defeated. Well, if you believe that, can you not wish to die in the charge rather than be cut down ignominiously from behind while you're flying away from conflict?"

Murray shook his head sadly.

"I'll command the rear myself," he said.

The prince gave up. The Stuart blood, high-charged with arrogance, showed at its worst. His highness's eyes were ungraciously afrown, and a sneer defaced the royal lips.

"It would seem that I must accept the dictation of my father's subjects. I am called a prince but I am made a servant. Well, I will order the retreat—since a refusal would find me deserted by men who want to run home."

He turned his back upon them and walked to the door. And there, as they had expected, he turned for a final word.

"The council is dismissed. This is the last council I shall summon. I had wanted you for advice and assistance, but I find you giving me insult instead. Hereafter, I command alone."

He quit the room, unattended. He slammed the door behind him.

The Young Lochiel took the news to Malcolm, at Mr. Littlehorse's house. Malcolm said nothing, and Lochiel left. Gillie Angus bustled in, to prepare his master for bed. Angus ordinarily was a model valet, but this night the thrill of a march to the great city had loosened his tongue and bent the formality he was wont to observe.

"They were talkin' aboot Lunnon City, Macdomhnull Dhu?"

"Aye."

"Did they decide which clan would be Bonnie Charlie's guard when we march in?"

Malcolm whirled upon him.

"Is it a general you've been made that you must know all this? I'll not be needing you to undress. Get out!"

Gillie Angus, astounded, but wisely prompt to obey, backed out of the room. His face, as the door closed upon it, carried an expression at once puzzled and sorrowful—the expression of a dog that has been whipped for something it does not understand.

Malcolm was instantly sorry. He went to the window and gazed out at the blacksmith's shop. It was early evening. The smith's grindstone was whirling, and there was a conical projection of sparks where it sped past the edge of a claymore. Ever since the entry into Derby the clansmen had been gathered at this shop, and, now that the question of precedence at last had been settled, the broadswords, in their proper order, were being sharpened as rapidly as the smith could sharpen them. It was well that the clansmen should be prepared to enter London. . . . Possibly they might find some resistance? The very thought made them laugh.

There were four of them around the grindstone still. One was Old Angus, piper for the Glenallan. His voice, high-pitched and broken by excitement, reached Malcolm at the window.

"Aye, Macdomhnull Dhu was only the second mon ta get in Edinbro'. Aye. That was because he slipped on a roun' stone, ye ken. But he will be the *first* mon ta get in Lunnon! There's no' can beat that laddie!"

CHAPTER 11

CAPTAIN FITZSTEPHEN OF THE dragoons had twice informed General Hawley that the Highlanders were advancing, and had twice been told to go to the devil.

It was not possible that the rebels would have the audacity to attack. They had their own hills at their backs: they knew when they were whipped. The Young Pretender was undoubtedly a fool, but General Hawley had never heard that he was a half-wit.

A storm was blowing up, and to continue the chase now would be foolish. Besides, the wine at Callander House was the best the general had tasted for many a day; the Countess Kilmarnock, for all the sad mistakes of her husband, was one of the most charming hostesses that ever lived; and so, in short, would Captain Fitzstephen please get out, sir, and not be so silly?

Thus reasoned General Hawley. But Fitzstephen thought differently on the matter, and he lingered.

Captain Fitzstephen was not happy. He had recently learned of the marriage of Helen Hornsby to the Laird of Glenallan. For a second time that young barbarian had come between the captain and his money, and that was a sin the captain could not forgive. To be sure, Glenallan would soon be killed—either in battle, or, when the rebellion had been snuffed out, on the scaffold—and Lady Helen, widowed, would undoubtedly become reconciled with her family. But she would not remarry. She'd make a martyr of the man. That's the kind of woman she was—romantic, impractical.

Fitzstephen was not romantic, and neither was he impractical. The news of the marriage jolted him, but he wasted no time grinding his teeth or thumping his breast. There was nothing lucrative about despair. He was busy with another thought now—a wild hope. He was, he knew, as well mounted as any man in the service of the king; and when the final fight came—and that would be soon—there might be a chance for him to break through the Scottish lines and reach the person of the Pretender. The man who captured the Pretender, or killed him, would be the hero of his generation. More important, he would win a reward of thirty thousand pounds. Fitzstephen could use the glory, but cash was the true stimulant.

It was, admittedly, a wild hope. But it was the only hope he had at this moment.

Because of this, he was impatient with Hawley. If the rebels were really advancing, as reported, then it was time to crush them. The victory would be cleaner, more complete, than a victory in the hills. Moreover, Fitzstephen was troubled about this "breakfast." It was near noon already. He peered again into the dining room.

It was a handsome room, square, large, paneled to the ceiling in walnut that was almost black from age; and there were small pilasters, with Corinthian capitals pricked out in gold, at the top of the paneling.

In the center was an enormous table at which the hostess and the general sat. Beauty and the Beast. Countess Kilmarnock was tall and handsome, voluptuously built, and very lovely to look at, dressed now in red silk and gold thread lace. She was all woman, with softly curved neck and shoulders, round white arms, small hands, a caressive voice. General Hawley was all man—a blustering, bellowing soldier, broad-shouldered, deep-chested, with a big sneering mouth and a high and haughty nose. His neck was thick, his body was toadlike, and his face was as red as the wine he drank.

"I tell you, ma'am, we're going to smash 'em to bits! Why, before I left Edinburgh, d'ye know what I did?"

The countess admitted that she did not know what he had done, and expressed great eagerness to learn.

Hawley unslipped the last button of his waistcoat, stretched his legs full-length under the table, and grinned.

"I had six gallows erected," he told her. "Six of 'em, ma'am! Lord, what a business they will do when I fetch the rebels back! They're dealing with a man now, not a figgety fop like Cope."

He drained his glass, and a flunky behind him, suspiciously prompt, refilled it.

The Countess Kilmarnock said: "Yes, surely they have a real man to deal with now. That must be why they are retreating."

Fitzstephen, peering in, marveled at her manner. No woman so accomplished could esteem Hawley an attractive figure—though this appeared to be the general's own explanation of the hospitality. Perhaps the countess, being a sensible woman, was already laying plans against the time when her husband would be sentenced to hang. Or, again, it could be that the countess was aware of the insurgents' plans and was deliberately trying to keep General Hawley from his camp, two miles away.

"They chased Cope away," Hawley explained, "and they got past Wade, and they even got past Cumberland. Oh, they can march! No question of that. But there's an end to this island, ma'am, and I'm going to shove them off."

A sergeant attached to his own company, on headquarters duty, approached Captain Fitzstephen. The sergeant had been riding hard; his uniform was wet, and his boots were splattered with mud.

"The rebels have been seen crossing the Carron at Dunnipace Steps. Colonel Ligonier told me to see that this news reached General Hawley personally, sir. He said it meant they're going to try to take the top of the moor."

Fitzstephen strode without hesitation into the dining room.

"Madam—sir—I hope you will forgive a third interruption—"

"Damn me! What is it this time?"

"Colonel Ligonier, sir, sends word that the rebels have

crossed the Carron and are trying to take the top of the moor."

Hawley shook his head as though to clear it, and brushed his hand across his eyes like a man who had walked into a cobweb.

"My horse!"

He rushed from the room, scarcely a leap behind Captain Fitzstephen, and without addressing another word to the woman whose charms had kept him so long from camp.

He found the camp in a turmoil. The colonels were grouped in anxious conference at their headquarters tent, afraid to move without the command of the general. Hawley stamped among them, hatless, wigless, his coat unbuttoned, his boots and breeches all mud.

"Ligonier, Hamilton—where the hell is Hamilton?—and you too, Cobham. Make all possible speed through that park and to the top of the moor. You first, sir, and you second, and you third. Go *now*, you blockheads! You'll have further orders before you get there."

Even his own aides had never seen him so boisterous, yet so clearheaded. He roared commands steadily, tolerating no interruption and no answer.

"Wolfe, are you ready? Good, sir! March your men immediately after the dragoons. Barrel, then Monro, then Scott . . ."

Scarcely twenty minutes after his arrival, an entire army had been set in motion, three regiments of dragoons galloping ahead, the foot regiments following, the artillery bringing up in the rear.

They splashed through Bantaskine Park and hurried up Maggie Wood's Lane.

There was a strong southwest wind blowing rain directly into their faces, and it was very dark.

Hawley, with water streaming down his face and the gay froggery of his coat in ludicrous disarray, charged back and forth at the head of his aides, never ceasing to bellow. His face was almost black with rage. The veins of his neck, bluish-green, stood out like fluting on a breastplate.

Captain Fitzstephen was in the van, riding like mad. Certainly the dragoons would charge. The dragoons traditionally were not cavalry but mounted infantry, horse soldiers; but they *were* mounted, they *were* in the van, and they were smarting still from the shame of Prestonpans, from which field the dragoons, without ever having been fired upon, had led the rout. Of course they'd charge today! And Captain Fitzstephen would charge at the head of them. It would be his opportunity, and he meant to seize it.

The top of Falkirk Moor was irregular and rocky, and a deep ravine cut down from the place where Fitzstephen first sighted the rebels.

"They must have wings," he muttered.

But they had been running hard; their ranks were not properly assembled; a cavalry charge, made with spirit, would throw them into confusion. Fitzstephen would have anticipated the command even if it had not reached him almost at the very instant when the tartaned warriors burst upon his view. He had already drawn his saber, which now he waved over his head, turning in saddle.

"With me, men! Not a one gets away!"

The Highlanders assembled quickly, the men from the rear scurrying forward to fill the gaps in the ranks, while those who had outstripped the others stepped hastily back. Their muskets and pistols were leveled at the onrushing dragoons. They waited. That was the odd part of it—they waited. By all the rules of warfare, they should have turned and run.

But they waited, motionless. And when the dragoons were less than half a pistol shot away, and not until then, the Highlanders fired.

The dragoons broke instantly. That single volley did it. Most of the horses, green animals, never trained to charge into gunsmoke, reared and stamped beyond control, or turned tail and dashed back among the foot soldiers.

Fitzstephen's steed was better taught, and Fitzstephen's own spirit was sounder. He tried desperately to rally his men, but they pretended that they could no longer control the horses, and the captain, after a few moments of vain shouting and saber waving, during which time a second volley emptied many more saddles, himself continued the charge. He hadn't gone mad, as the Highlanders supposed, nor was his mount out of control. He simply reasoned that it was not possible that the other companies had acted as disgracefully as his own. Because of the rain and the darkness and the smoke, he had only been able to see those immediately about him.

So he charged alone, one man against an army.

A Wild Scot stepped into his path, flourishing a broadsword—and leaped out of the way barely in time to save himself from being trampled. Another tried to drag the captain from his saddle—and received a saber cut that laid his head open. A third, a short, empty-faced fellow, caught Fitzstephen's coat with the hook end of a Lochaber ax and yanked the captain to the ground. Before Fitzstephen had a chance to move, the Scot dropped his ax and leaped upon him. And Fitzstephen, with a poinard at his throat, did not stir.

"Why don't you kill me?" he suggested coldly.

Apparently the Highlandman did not understand English. He shook his head, his face assuming an expression of even more than ordinary bewilderment. His knee still pressing the captain's chest, he recovered the captain's pistol with his left hand and then he rose to his feet.

There seemed to be little fighting around them. Most of

the Scots had moved forward, and they were firing their
pieces occasionally. Some of them had drawn their swords
and swung their targets into position, but they did not move.
The truth was, they couldn't believe that men could be so
cowardly as the dragoons, and they paused, smelling a trap.

The blank-faced Highlander conducted Fitzstephen to the
front rank, covering him carefully with the pistol all the
while. There he muttered a few words to a dark, excited
young man, evidently a gentleman, who had been using all
his power to prevent the men around him from dashing down
the hill into what might well be death. The young man
nodded, and presently addressed Fitzstephen.

"You are a prisoner, sir."

"So it seems. May I ask *whose?*"

It sounded very medieval; but then, he was among medi-
eval-minded men.

"The prisoner of my chief, sir."

"And he is?"

The young man considered this for a moment, thoughtfully, and then nodded as though to indicate that he found
the question a fair one. He turned away, and engaged in
whispered conversation with another, somewhat taller young
man. And soon this second young man turned to face Captain
Fitzstephen.

"You are the prisoner, sir, of Sir Malcolm MacIldowie
Macdomhnull Dhu, the Laird of Glenallan and chief of the
clan of that ilk."

"Well, I'll be damned! My old gambling friend!"

They stared at one another for perhaps a full minute,
while Old Angus piped loudly and yelling men ran here
and there. They did not move. Long thin wisps of smoke
floated between their faces, and there was a distant rattle of
musketry on the right. Evan of Lochallan, instantly aware of

something unusual about this meeting, watched the two men carefully.

The captain was the first to speak. He straightened his coat with two downward jerks.

"How fortunate that I should fall into the hands of one who loves me so dearly."

Malcolm turned to Dafty.

"Tie his hands and take him back to town. I make you responsible for him."

"I suppose you will hang me?" Fitzstephen asked.

Malcolm shook his head.

"If I'm killed, you become a prisoner of war, and Prince Charles may do as he pleases with you. But he won't kill you, no."

Fitzstephen would have made some sharp retort, but Dafty led him away; and the Glenallan clan remained in its position in the front line, waiting for the order to advance.

The battle of Falkirk, as far as the Glenallans were concerned, was no more than a skirmish. By the time they had been commanded to charge, the enemy had retreated beyond reach. Some of the Englishmen, it is true, were found in the town, and these were cut down without mercy. Others, dragoons, had galloped the whole length of the Highland line in their panic, and had been decimated by a running fire. Still other dragoons had retreated wildly among the foot soldiers, trampling many of these, and throwing them into confusion. The cannon had been mired at the foot of Maggie Wood's Lane.

If the Highlanders had charged promptly, Hawley would have had no troops to lead in retreat. As it was, only the right wing advanced. There was no holding the Macdonalds: they were too hot for battle to be restrained by mere military commands. They fought like demons, and almost succeeded in cutting off the enemy's escape. Hawley's camp was captured, together with all his baggage, and his military chest. And Hawley himself, spectacularly baffled, fell back to the safety of Edinburgh—where there were six stout gallows to mock him.

As for Malcolm, he was well pleased that the conflict had been so brief. Revenge upon Captain Fitzstephen occupied his mind entirely. He was more than usually taciturn, and every delay in reassembling the men stirred him to harsh impatience. But he got permission to quit the field early, and he returned to Stirling.

The captain's horse, tied to a hitching post, was the first thing that he observed when he turned into the street in which Mr. Montcrief's house stood. Fitzstephen, wrists tied, was seated in a corner of Malcolm's bedroom, the English pistol that the half-wit held still pointed at his breast. Outside in the hall were Mr. Montcrief and his wife, alarmed but at the same time very inquisitive. Dafty would not permit them to enter.

The laird was attended only by Evan of Lochallan, to whom he had explained everything. He gazed thoughtfully upon his captive.

Fitzstephen demanded petulantly: "How long are you going to keep me here?"

"It's too dark to fight now."

"Ah!" The captain looked up with more interest. "You're still bent on a rencontre?"

"Aye."

Fitzstephen shrugged, smiled, made a mock bow, and indicated by his expression that such a meeting would not be unwelcome. But he asked again if he were to be kept tied, remarking that this position would cramp his muscles and probably prevent him from being in proper condition when he went to the field of honor.

"That is fair," said Malcolm, and he commanded Dafty to

untie the prisoner, at the same time instructing the half-wit to remain on watch. To Fitzstephen he said, in English: "You preferred small swords, court swords. There are none of those here. At least, none we could borrow without raising suspicion, and dueling has been strictly forbidden by the prince. We must make other arrangements."

"A walking armory like you should not be at a loss. Those pistols—"

Malcolm unhooked the pistols from his belt, knocked the powder and ball from them, and laid them on the table. But he shook his head. They were good dags, very long, made of iron and steel, with unguarded ball triggers and screw barrels. But they would hardly do for dueling. They were not equipped with sights, and they were not perfectly mated.

If the captain desired them, all right. But Malcolm knew that his cousin, who would act as his representative, possessed the best dueling pistols in Scotland, a pair of rifled Williamesons. These would be sent to the captain for his inspection and approval.

"You're very kind. It might interest you to know," said Fitzstephen, "that I am considered one of the best shots in His Majesty's service."

"Daybreak will be a good time?"

"Any time will be a good time to kill you, Jocky."

"I shall see that you have seconds. I shall make the other arrangements."

Fitzstephen shrugged and turned away. In spite of himself, Malcolm could not help admiring the man's courage. He bowed stiffly, glanced again at Dafty, and started out of the room.

"Must I be entertained by this moonface all night?" asked Fitzstephen.

"You must."

"Won't you take my parole?"

"No."

Fitzstephen was exasperated.

"Have you no respect at all for my word of honor as a gentleman?"

"None at all," said Malcolm, and quit the room.

Young Lochiel, when he returned from the field, consented to the use of his Williamesons and consented also to act as a second. Malcolm conferred at length with him, in Donald's room just across the street. It was decided that Lochiel and Bobby MacUalrig would act for Fitzstephen, as a formality, and that Lochallan and Evan Macgregor, a major now, would act for Malcolm.

MacUalrig produced the weapons, in a rosewood box, and Malcolm handled them lovingly. He would have given half his property for them, but he knew that nothing could induce Donald to sell them. They were exactly alike—flat-plated, flat-cocked, with silver ramrods, real Damascus twist barrels, and butts of close-grained Circassian walnut inlaid with silver wire scrolls. Their balance was perfect, their sights the finest ever made. They were sent to Captain Fitzstephen, who kept them for nearly an hour, returning them at last, by Bobby MacUalrig, with the message that they were in every way satisfactory.

Fitzstephen was to occupy Malcolm's room for the night, while the young laird slept with his cousin.

In the darkness, Donald talked about the battle, the magnificent spirit of the Macdonalds, and the hard feeling among the chiefs because they were no longer called into council. He had never been more loquacious, even in Malcolm's presence. But he said not a word about the coming duel. He was not happy about it—this Malcolm knew. He had offered no word of objection, knowing Malcolm too well to suppose that objections would be heeded. But nevertheless he didn't like the business. At best, it would mean many apologies and explanations in the prince's presence, and possibly disgrace for all of them, for Charles had been in an ugly humor since Derby and was not likely to excuse the settlement of personal differences at a time like this. At worst, it would mean Callum MacIldowie's death.

"You've not heard from your wife at all, Callum?"

"Nay."

"Are ye no' worried?"

"Aye."

Of course she could not get a letter to him: Edinburgh was in the hands of the German's men. His common sense as well as his knowledge of military matters might have reassured Malcolm. But at the thought that he might never see Helen again he felt a fear stronger, more definite, infinitely more terrible, than the fear that had passed over him just before the charge at Prestonpans.

He shouldn't worry like this. He needed sleep.

He decided to pray. It was not often that he prayed. After some especially remarkable exhibition of the Creator's might, he believed, a prayer was decent and acceptable to Heaven. But it was only in extraordinary circumstances that Malcolm asked for help in trouble; for that, he believed, argued a lack of confidence and faith. He had his own ideas about faith.

He moved his lips in the darkness, saying the words in his mind but not aloud, for fear of waking Donald. . . .

It was still dark when one of Donald's gillies awakened them. The Cameron dressed quickly and took his customary morning drink—two fingers of brandy. Malcolm's morning drink was three fingers. Neither ate any food: it was well that Malcolm should go to the meeting with an empty stomach. Bobby MacUalrig, always to be found somewhere near his chief, was quartered in the same house; and he joined them quietly, the pistol case under his arm. They were to meet Macgregor and Lochallan on the field.

There was no conversation. Donald of Lochiel, faced with the prospect of witnessing the death of the man to whom, after his father the chief, he gave the greatest love, had need of all the courage that was in him.

The faithful MacUalrig admired Malcolm as a warrior, and respected him as a descendant of Donald the Black and of Aonghas; but MacUalrig was most concerned over the trouble in which his chief was likely to find himself. The prince would not like this business. He would complain that it would give the English another monstrous lie about the mistreatment of prisoners by the rebels. He would be angry with the Young Lochiel.

There was the Glenallan clan to consider too. If Callum and not the Englishman were killed, the Glenallans might be willing to follow a representative of the House of Lochiel or the House of Letterfinlay; but certainly none of them would do so while Fitzstephen lived. For the Glenallans, as MacUalrig knew, were fighting not for the glory of the Stuart but for the glory of their own chief, their beloved Macdomhnull Dhu. And so Bobby MacUalrig shook his head.

Malcolm himself gave no indication that the matter troubled him. But then, it was always difficult to tell what Malcolm's feelings might be. He was clear-eyed and expressionless this morning. He seemed to have slept well.

They had their first premonition of trouble when they descended into the bleak gray street, still dark. Captain Fitzstephen's horse, a blooded beast, beautifully built, was not tied to the hitching post at the side of Mr. Montcrief's house. Malcolm remarked it instantly.

"Ye ken, Donald, I commanded that the animal stay there all night."

"Aye."

Mr. Montcrief admitted them quietly. He knew of nothing wrong, he said. There had not been a sound from Fitzstephen's room all night—though Mr. Montcrief could not vouch for the time, perhaps two hours, during which he dozed. The horse? Somebody must have stolen the horse. It had been reckless anyway, leaving so expensive an animal practically in the street all night.

But Malcolm and his cousin were convinced that there had been trouble. They went up the steps three at a time, and so into the bedroom.

Dafty was seated where they had left him, but he was doubled over his face upon his knees, his hands, palms up, just touching the floor. He was naked except for an undershirt. Blood that had dried was on his lower legs and on the floor between his feet.

They straightened him in the chair. His throat had been cut from ear to ear, evidently with his own dirk, which, covered with blood, lay on the floor nearby. The pistol was gone. A note was on the table:

> *You must not think I was afraid. When the simpleton snoozed, I only did what any sensible man would do. You will find an excellent dragoon captain's uniform under the bed. It is yours: permit me to recommend it in place of these damned skirts.*

—F<small>ITZ</small>

CHAPTER 12

I<small>T WAS ON THE LAST DAY OF</small> January that the Duke of Cumberland, at the head of ten thousand men, quit Edinburgh to disperse the rebels.

The soldiers called him Bluff Bill. He was a young man—just Charles Edward's age, twenty-four. And like Charles Edward, he had plenty of natural courage. But where comparison was inevitable, there was no other point of resemblance. His Royal Highness of Cumberland was thick-faced, thick-necked, stolid. He had been raised in the military tradition of the Germans, and had no respect for human kindness and no patience with worn-out notions of chivalry.

From the drawing room of Robert Forbes' house Lady Helen of Glenallan watched him pass. She had met him many times at court, for he was the king's second son, and she hated him. He was rude, brutal, ugly. Yet it was said that he was a great soldier, and she sighed as she watched him go.

She saw him raise a gloved hand to his bonnet, smiling to right and left. Smiling? It was rather a mean grin. It seemed to say to the crowds: "You'd damned well better cheer me! The side of the hangman is the side a wise man prefers." So he went out of the city; and Lady Helen, like every other person in Edinburgh, was remembering the time when Bonnie Prince Charlie had gone forth at the head of his men, and the way Prince Charlie had smiled. . . .

She was heavyhearted. She knew that there was good foundation for Cumberland's confidence. The clans were cornered, without hope of further supplies, and terribly outnumbered. Some Jacobites still insisted that nothing was impossible to a man so brave and so ingenious as the Stuart; but Lady Helen, for all her devotion to her husband's cause, knew that the end was near. She could feel it. As before a storm the air is still, the grass lies flat, and birds and other animals disappear silently, so before the final battle all Edinburgh held its breath.

She was lonesome now. There was no activity at Holyroodhouse. Her friends were cool. Gerald was alternately cold and loud with abuse. Robert Forbes, always the host, was embarrassed: the viscount was angry about the marriage, and the viscount was Robert Forbes' friend and benefactor. Lady Helen was a stranger among her own people. Already she belonged to those hills she had never seen.

But she continued to stay at the house in the Cannongate. There was nothing else to do—except return to London, and this she refused to consider.

"He'll be killed," Gerald told her many times. "Either he'll be killed in the big fight coming or else he'll be caught and hanged."

Nevertheless she stayed in Edinburgh and continued to hope. Prince Charles, she feared, was doomed. But they would have no easy time taking Malcolm's life. Malcolm was tough and quick and strong. The confidence she had in her husband was all that was left to Lady Helen. She sat, many hours of the day, in the window seat where they had talked in the past. She could close her eyes and see him stride up and down the room, frowning because the words that he wanted would not come to him, impatient and angry as though those words were tardy servants. She could see him, all steel and silver, standing before the fireplace, a fitting foreground for the panoply of weapons there. She could see him beside her in the window seat, staring at her as a man might stare at a vision from Heaven.

The snows began to go. The spring rains washed the white from the hills as though it had been so much talk. The streams of Scotland became obstreperous and very busy; where there had been rivulets, rivers appeared, and the ground that had been frozen hard as rock became soft with mud and slush.

There were no supplies for the starving Highlanders around Inverness. Lord George Murray was called back from the Athole country. Lochiel was called in from the siege of Fort Augustus. And messengers were sent to scour the hills for the foraging parties that were active everywhere.

On the fourteenth of April a gillie brought news that

Cumberland had crossed the Spey and was advancing rapidly. Prince Charles, on the following day, rallied his men—such of them as could be found—and marched them out on Drummossie Muir. To their right was the river Nairn, to the left Culloden 'House and the sea; and behind them, glaring back, were the Highlands.

They might retreat farther and scatter among the hills, to be hunted out like little animals. Or they might stand their ground and be slaughtered.

No, there was one other chance, one last chance. Lord George Murray proposed it.

"Nothing but a miracle will save us if we remain here, and Your Highness is aware that to depend upon miracles is poor military policy."

"I will not retreat again. Let the world say I'm a fool. It shall never say I am a coward."

Lord George bowed.

"I was thinking, Sire, of your royal father."

"Retreat would not help my father."

"I believe that to be true. But there is another course. It is a desperate one, but it's better than waiting for that miracle. Cumberland's men are eighteen miles away, as Your Highness knows. They will resume their march in the morning—but not early, for they marched hard today. Tonight they will sleep well. For another army, eighteen miles on a night like this would not be possible. But Your Highness's men have done it before, and they could do it again. May I submit—the last thing anybody would expect of us—a night attack?"

There was a high wind, and it was bitter cold. The van encountered frozen water and mud, and left sharp broken chunks of ice floating in the puddles to cut the brogues and the feet of those who followed. For twenty-four hours they had eaten no food, and they were so tired that they could scarcely swing their legs. Man after man fell by the way. Some of them froze to death, some starved to death.

The Glenallan said to his men, as they marched: "You're to be silent till I give the command to charge. Then use your claymores—no pistols or muskets. Rush down among the tents, and wherever you see a hump, stick it. Yell all the time. And Angus, I want you to blow up as you've never blown before."

Lochallan's gillie fell. His bare feet were frozen. David MacMichael lifted the man on his own mighty shoulders, and carried him.

By the time the Saxon camp was sighted, dawn had come. The main part of the army had still to appear; some of the companies were several miles back; and Lord George Murray shook his head. It would be as sensible to have all the men throw themselves into the sea as to have them attack now. The chance had gone. The best they could do was return to their original position and wait for their fate. He gave the command to retreat.

Through the sticky mud, in the light of a sickly dawn, they staggered back. Many never got there. Where one man had fallen previously, three fell now. That icy wind brought death as surely as though it had been a shower of bullets. There was no longer any attempt to carry the frozen men. Great Davie's burden became cold on Davie's back.

"The mon's dead, ye loony!"

So Lochallan's gillie was dropped by the roadside, and the Glenallans staggered on, cursing sometimes, and sometimes praying, but most of the time grimly silent. And Malcolm walked at the head of them, with Evan of Lochallan on his right side, Walter MacPhail on his left.

The duke's men came on, colors flying, bayonets gleam-

ing, drums athunder, white gaiters swinging regularly as the
men marched—a grand mass of steel and scarlet, moving
with the precision of a machine. About a mile away they
halted to reform their lines.

"I don't like it, Callum," said Donald of Lochiel. "They're
on higher ground, and the wind's at our faces. When the
firing starts, we'll be blind for the smoke."

"Aye."

There was still more moving to be done. The Glenallans
were shifted and shifted, without any apparent reason; they
dragged themselves back and forth, obedient, leaden-
legged; and in the end they found themselves just where
they had been in the morning. But at least the motion served
to keep the men awake.

On the tip of the right wing were the warriors from
Athole. The Glenallans were placed next to them, the Cam-
erons next, and beyond the Camerons were the Stewarts of
Appine, the Frazers, the MacIntoshes, the Farquharsons, the
Chisholms, the Duke of Perth's men, Roy Stewart's men, and
the Macdonalds.

Why the Macdonalds were on the left wing was a mystery. Since Bannockburn their place had always been on the
right; that position was theirs by all tradition. They were
angry at the change, and they showed it.

The sun had been out earlier, but now black clouds were
spreading; the wind stiffened and was wet and sharp and
very cold; soon the rain began to fall.

In all the clans, and in the second line, the gentlemen,
with drawn swords, harangued the warriors, or they passed
in and out between the ranks, shouting encouragement.

"Scrug your bonnets, laddies! We'll read the riot act to
them this time!"

Only the expectation of a charge kept the men on their
feet. And even with this there were many who could not

stand, so worn were they and so hungry; they lay on their backs, moaning, begging for food.

Messengers hurried here and there, sometimes rising in their stirrups the better to glimpse the scarlet host across the moor.

"A half pint of whisky for each man, and a single bannock apiece, and we'd be sure of it," Lochiel said to his cousin.

"You could even leave out the bannock," said Donald. "The laddies are near kilt with the cold."

The prince went by, on a beautiful black Spanish jennet. He waved cheerfully at Lochiel and at Malcolm, and smiled encouragement. The chances were a thousand to one against him, but he was as gay and as smart as ever he had been in Holyroodhouse while leading a lady through a minuet. Tall white feathers nodded on his bonnet.

"They're comin' ag'in," Gillie Angus remarked.

The duke's men moved still farther forward, until they were almost within gunshot. The Highlanders, excited at first, were dismayed when they saw the halt. Why was there no command to charge? Did Charlie think that they could stand forever and watch those banners wave and listen to the beating of those damned drums?

Down near the center two pipers blew up and some men sang a little; but this soon died, and there was a long pause —a heavy, horrid silence.

Then the cannon near the center exploded with a roar, and smoke blotted the enemy from sight. Almost immediately the Saxon cannon, which were much more numerous, opened return fire. The smoke was redoubled. The noise was terrific. Some of the men threw themselves on the ground, covering their heads with their arms in an effort to protect their ears; but the gentlemen were among them always, cursing, threatening, pleading.

The rain came down with increasing sharpness. The drops, which were very large, struck like pellets of lead.

Still there was no command to advance. The Glenallan men, though better behaved, were as restless as the Camerons and the Athole men, and as anxious for a charge.

"Must we stand here and be blown up by machines?" their eyes seemed to say.

The laird himself flipped up bits of turf with the point of his sword, and he frowned upon the ground, swearing softly.

An aide shook his shoulder, shouted into his ear.

"There may be a rumor the prince was killed—deny it!" Malcolm grabbed the reins.

"It's a lie, man? For the sake of God, it's a lie!"

"Yes, yes! Let my horse go! He's safe. Deny it! A ball splashed him with mud, that's all."

And he rode away.

The Glenallan clansmen looked a question at their chief, but he shook an impatient head to indicate that the matter was none of their business.

It seemed as though the firing continued for hours. Because of the smoke, it was impossible to see the sky. Most of the men thought that night had come. They fingered the triggers of their muskets, and a few fired from bravado; they loosened their claymores; they pulled their bonnets far down over their foreheads.

A cannon ball screamed through the ranks not ten feet from the chief. Somebody shrieked. Malcolm felt his way around as a man in fog might do, and learned that Walter MacPhail was dead, ripped to pieces, while Paul Mac-Michael hopped foolishly about, holding cupped hands over a nasty red blotch on his right leg.

Evan of Lochallan grabbed Malcolm's arm and pointed to the Camerons. The Camerons, giving their war cry, were rushing into the thickest smoke. Malcolm could not hear them, but he could see their mouths move, and their faces were twisted by hate. There had been no order to charge; but Malcolm could not watch his cousins dash at the enemy and leave them behind. He raised his sword.

"Claymores! Claymores!"

"*Glenallan!*" the men yelled.

Muskets were crashing on the left now, where the Camerons were, but there was no sound of firing from the Macdonald end of the line.

He bent far down, holding his target over his head and running with all the speed in his legs. . . . He came through the smoke abruptly and met the Englishmen.

They were three deep. Malcolm sent one to the ground with a blow that almost took the man's arm off at the shoulder. He lifted aside a bayonet and thrust at a bright red coat—but even as he did so he slipped on the wet ground and was kicked in the face.

He rose without an instant's pause, and was cutting right and left, his target still held high. And in less than a minute there was nobody before him and he was leading his men against the second line.

Again three deep the redcoats waited. They did not move. They were less than a hundred feet away, and Malcolm ran with all the speed that was in him—but they did not move. The triple row of muskets faced him motionlessly, as though they were that many sticks protruding from a stone wall. Why didn't they fire? *Why didn't they fire?* It seemed as though his legs were made of iron. The mud was as sticky as glue, and the distance lessened very slowly.

Then the air was all smoke again. Malcolm found himself on the ground, spitting mud, reaching for the sword that had somehow been wrenched from his hand. He rose to one knee and was hit in the left shoulder with a musket stock. He rolled, rose again—and found himself confronting a redcoat. For an instant the two men stared wildly at each other, their noses not more than three inches apart. Then Malcolm flashed out a dirk, and the redcoat flapped his arms, worked his mouth open and shut as though he would talk, and fell to the ground.

"*Glenallan! Glenallan!*"

He could no longer hear the pipes, and that was ominous. He ran short distances here and there, looking for his claymore. A redcoat rushed up to him, but turned tail when Malcolm lifted the dirk. Another redcoat, his hands around a musket barrel, stood nearby and dared Malcolm to approach him. But there were no Highlanders in sight.

At last he found the claymore—the genuine Andrea Ferrara. He turned and looked around him.

He was on a high place. He remembered that the charge had been made up a hill, but he had not realized he'd come so far. A breeze had lifted most of the smoke away. Running toward the distant black mountains and toward the swollen Nairn, stumbling, wailing, dragging their weapons behind them and throwing them away altogether, were the Highland clansmen. Here and there a company was orderly and marched with some semblance of military rule, stopping occasionally to fire at their pursuers, and loading again before they continued the retreat. Here and there a small group, pursued too enthusiastically, turned with the ferocity of true desperation and fought it out on the spot until it was cut down entirely.

But most of the laddies were broken with despair and concerned only with getting away. On both wings there were cavalrymen, shouting in triumph, slashing with their sabers, rising and falling as their horses heaved. The cannon were deserted. The prince was not in sight.

Malcolm saw the Camerons now, on slightly lower ground, backing away before a series of rushes that the redcoats were making. He saw a group around the battle standard; the finest men were there, for Malcolm could make out the eagle feathers in their bonnets and he saw the brave swing of their swords. They surrounded a man who was on the ground, and they were fighting with a grand ferocity.

And this was the end of Prince Charlie's hopes, and probably the end of Charlie himself. The glory was gone. It was only slaughter that remained, and dirty retreating, the insolence of the Southron. There were tears in the Glenallan's eyes and black despair in his heart as he viewed the scene.

But now the redcoat who held the clubbed musket, and who had been acting like a quarrelsome, frightened boy, was joined by another, and they rushed at him, the second man with his bayonet forward.

"Ye mongrels!"

He dropped to one knee, threw the bayonet off, and returned a blow at the head that sent the second soldier staggering backward.

But there were other redcoats coming, from behind these two.

The man with the clubbed musket lost courage suddenly— and then, when he saw that he was reinforced, as suddenly regained it. For a minute there was such fighting that the laird did not know which direction he faced nor how many men he had struck. Nor did he realize that he himself had been struck and was bleeding. But somebody was fighting next to him—that much he did know. And when the redcoats stepped back, amazed and frightened by the fury with which they had been met, Malcolm turned to embrace faithful Evan of Lochallan.

"Where are the men?"

Evan shook his head.

"I saw Old Angus killed—"

He took Malcolm's arm and pointed toward the Camerons, and particularly toward the ground that surrounded the fallen man.

"The tall one—"

It was Robert MacUalrig, enormous Bobby, who never left his chief's side. Malcolm felt sick at the sight. It could only mean that Donald of Lochiel was down.

"Come on!"

Evan nodded, and the two of them ran down the slope toward the Cameron stand. There was the Young Lochiel, eyes open and brightly flashing, but with a face that was pale as death. He lay on his back, seemingly unable to rise, though there was no wound evident on him. He smiled when he saw Malcolm—his old smile.

"The Macdonalds didn't move, Callum."

Angus MacClarke and MacMartin of Letterfinlay appealed to the Glenallan. Donald would not permit them to carry him away. It was certain death if they tried to hold this place, when everybody else had run. Could not his cousin remonstrate with him? Malcolm agreed.

"We must move, Donald. We must get over the river."

"Retreat?"

"We must, Donald."

"Aye. Well, you know best."

The men made a sort of litter from muskets and plaids, and Donald was lifted onto this. His standard was still above him. His clansmen were two deep in back, Bobby MacUalrig towering above the others. And in this order the retreat began.

It was a perilous business. They could not go fast, because Donald was tortured with pain and every movement of the litter forced to his mouth a scream that never passed his teeth. Until they reached the Nairn, swollen high in this season, ice-clogged and rushing seaward with a roar, they were not seriously disturbed.

Malcolm and Evan and MacUalrig marched backward, claymores always ready, targets high. The men who were carrying the litter knew where they were going. Malcolm and Evan and MacUalrig only knew that they would get there, if the life of every man but Lochiel himself paid for it. The redcoats were not anxious to attack. Several gentlemen from other clans, cut off and lost as Malcolm had been, joined this group as it proceeded along the river bank. They were the men who had penetrated farthest into the enemy ranks, the bravest, the most desperate.

Most of the redcoats, battle-weary, contented themselves with chasing and cutting down those Highlanders who were not so determined. But there were a few who were inspired to command an attack against this group, for they saw the Lochiel standard. Fortunately, none of these had a charge left in his musket, and the rain had wetted their powder, so that the fighting was all with bayonet and sword.

Malcolm was heartened, just before the river was reached, by the arrival of Great Davie, who joined the company as quietly as though nothing unusual had happened that day, and took his place on Malcolm's left, Evan of Lochallan being on the right.

"You're wounded," Great Davie told him, without looking around. "You're bleedin' bad in the shoulder there."

"Aye. That's for later. Watch that tall fellow. He's got his back up for us."

They walked slowly along the river bank, pursued, generally at a respectful distance, by some thirty or forty foot soldiers, a group roughly equal to their own in numbers. The Lochiel banner, wet with rain, drooped woefully, like the Stuart hopes.

"Where is Gillie Angus?" Malcolm asked.

"Kilt."

"Where is Paul?"

"I fear he's killed too," Evan of Lochallan said. "He fell against me when we first charged. He wanted to run too, but he could no' stand."

"My brother John—he's kilt too," Great Davie offered. "I saw him drop. He was just ahead o' me. A good runner, John was. Two o' the *siler roy* hit him on the head wi' their muskets. I saw him, but I could no' get to where he was."

"Aye," said Evan. "I saw John fall. He was all over blood."

They had reached a ford. But it would be difficult to cross with the litter. Young Lochiel had fainted from pain—fainted without giving a groan. And a company of cavalry approached, flourishing their sabers and riding straight toward the defenders. They were brave enough, now that victory was won; but their horses must have been new to battle, for they reared and stamped when they got close to the Highlanders.

"Hit 'em on the nose! On the nose, laddies!"

There was a minute of terrible stamping and slashing, and then the cavalrymen were gone, intent upon easier prey. Three warriors of the breacan were on the ground, one of them Evan of Lochallan, whose ribs had been crushed by the hoofs of a horse, and who was dead.

"A braw man," said Bobby MacUalrig. "We needed him, too."

There was not time for lamentation. The cavalrymen, thinking better of it—perhaps thinking that the man on the litter, the man who was so well guarded, was Prince Charles himself—dismounted a short distance away; and with as many of the foot soldiers as they could induce to go with them, they started another and slower advance.

It would be impossible to cross the river now. It would mean that every Highlander would be killed. They decided to let the litter cross, four men supporting it, and hold this ford as long as they could. Donald must be given a good start.

They were solemn about the business. They kept close together, in a single line, feet spread wide apart and just enough room between the men for the proper swing of a broadsword.

"God be with us!" cried Bobby MacUalrig. "God grant that we hold 'em long enough!"

"Amen," said Malcolm.

Malcolm was backed against a little tree. He needed that support. He was horribly dizzy now; but whether this dizziness was caused by the exertions he had been undergoing, or by the almost constant clash of steel that was ringing in his ears, or by his wound—this he did not know. Perhaps it was caused by a realization of the disaster, a realization not yet fully come upon him but which was pressing against his temples like a vise. *Ochon!* The gallant Glenallans were lifeless lumps back there, and the gay Glenallan tartan was black with mud and blood and trampled down entirely. Only Great Davie stood by his side—his right side now—and he and Great Davie were waiting to be skewered.

He felt no pain in his body, though he had seen the shoulder wound and knew it was a bad one. But, indeed, he had no feeling of any sort. The numbness that had been his before the battle, when hunger and cold had seemed to cut his nerves, was back in him here at the ford. He saw the red soldiers coming closer, and he learned with alarm that he could not lift claymore and target together. He was too weak. He'd have to stand exposed, and let them hack him, pin him against the tree behind him. The thought made him wild. He dropped the target and managed to lift the broadsword with his two hands.

He got that blade up barely in time. The first to attack him was a powerful brute, with plenty of courage though little skill. Malcolm parried a head blow and returned a cut to the shoulder. The redcoat dropped his weapon, and, wheeling around, stumbled away. But he should have been killed. He had left a big opening. Malcolm knew that his strength was ebbing. He pressed hard against the tree.

The second man was a hatless, wigless fellow who shrieked as he came. Close behind him was another and bigger man.

A blow was aimed at Malcolm's left shoulder. He parried, but not with sufficient strength to entirely break the weight of the blow, so that the tip of the saber hit him gently. It must have touched the wound, for he felt a sharp sting there. He returned a flank blow, which, to his amazement, was parried. He was slow! He feinted for the head and struck again at the flank, and this time the Saxon jumped back in sudden terror.

Meanwhile, the second man struck for the right shoulder. Malcolm could not parry in time, but he bent his knees and was not badly cut. He thrust straight for return, sticking the fellow neatly. But that left his head unprotected.

He was down, definitely down. He didn't know how he'd got there.

It was very hard getting to his feet again. If only he could have held up his target. . . . He knew he had been hit repeatedly, but the blows were not coming as fast as they should have come. Somebody was trying to protect him, cover him. That would be Great Davie.

He struggled furiously to get up, but his hands slipped in the slime, and he could not stiffen his knees. He believed that he could still swing the claymore if only he could get to his feet. All he needed was his right arm, and his sword. . . .

But there were his pistols. He had forgotten about them. He tried to find them with his hand. . . .

CHAPTER 13

Inverness, never noisy, had been frozen to silence by the breath of fear. The citizens were afraid to walk, all but afraid to talk; for there were redcoats everywhere.

Since the battle there had not been a sign of resistance. But England, frightened, was angry. The honor of English arms must be restored, somehow; and you never could trust these damned rebels, who were quiet today and screaming war cries tomorrow.

So Inverness, itself innocent, was still.

Lately the presence of a tall woman with beautiful clothes had excited no little suspicion and alarm among the citizens. It was whispered that she was a spy sent to learn the whereabouts of Charlie. She was too well dressed to be decent, too eager to talk to be guiltless of a deep design. However, if spy she was, they told one another, she was a poor one; for she could not speak above a dozen words of the Gaelic.

She came down the street, holding her cloak tight about her, stepping carefully between the puddles with her satin-slippered feet. There was some bewilderment and much anxiety in her face. She passed a redcoat, who idled off-duty before Luckie Anderson's place, and she approached two old men.

"Do you speak English?"

They shook their heads. They did speak a little English, both of them, but they preferred to deny this. Ignorance was the best policy in Inverness.

The woman held out a bit of dress breacan, vivid and impressive, clearly cut from the garb of a gentleman. Blocked from oral discourse, she asked with her eyes whether the two old men knew this design. But they only shook their heads again, edging away.

Another old man was passing—the only men left in Inverness were old men. The tall lady stopped him.

"Have you ever seen this? Do you know the man who wore it?"

He too shook his head. He glanced nervously at the redcoat. He hobbled on.

An old woman, brown and dour, her face multitudinously wrinkled, her eyes bright and very small, came out of Luckie Anderson's place—and the tall English lady accosted her too. But the old woman shook her head. No, she had never seen that breacan.

It was so in every case. They did not know the tartan, or they would not admit that they knew it, being afraid of the soldiers. Lady Helen turned away with a sigh. Two days in the town, two miserable days, after a difficult and dangerous trip from the city, had gained her no scrap of knowledge about her husband. She did not even know whether he was dead or alive.

Drooping with despair, she turned back toward the inn. The old woman got in her way.

"Let me see it again—"

Lady Helen presented the bit of plaid eagerly. The old woman examined it, turning it over, feeling it. At last she nodded.

"Aye, it was a tall laddie, bonnily built? Black hair he had, an' proud black eyes?"

There was something of the witch about this hag. She was thin, and her features were shrewd and sharp. Her little eyes glittered like the eyes of a snake. Lady Helen trembled. But she asked quickly:

"Have you seen him? Where is he?"

The old woman shook her head again, clucking her tongue against the roof of her mouth.

"Kilt."

"Killed! In the battle?"

"Aye."

There was a faraway roaring, as of thunder. The frowning north hills rolled down over her. The black sky seemed to settle swiftly upon her, engulfing her in darkness. The little street, the two old men, the hag, were obliterated. Lady Helen felt that she was dying. She leaned against a wall.

This passed, but it left her dizzy and sick. The old woman was walking away—walking with a straight, firm stride, a stride amazingly strong for a person of her years. Lady Helen pursued, running, and caught up with her. She took the old woman by the arm.

"Are you sure?"

The brown, many-wrinkled face was turned up again, and there was deep suspicion in the eyes.

"Did I no' see wi' my own eyne? He was cold there on the river bank, an' blood a' o'er him."

"You were on the battlefield, afterward?"

"Aye."

"And he was dead? You're sure?"

"Did I no' see him?" the old woman repeated angrily. "I dinna need the plaidie t' ken. 'Twas Macdomhnull Dhu, and dead as the dirt he was, like mony another braw laddie that day. Aye."

She nodded, peering into the tall lady's face, frowning; and then, suddenly, she resumed her stride and was gone.

Lady Helen walked slowly back to the inn. She went to her room on the second floor. It was a small room, dim and dirty. There was no fireplace, and in lieu of glass panes there were thin wooden shutters at the windows. There was no table, not even a chair, but a low, mean bed, and on the floor a bottle into the neck of which had been thrust a tallow candle.

She sat on the bed. Her feet were wet, but she did not

remove her slippers. She kept her cloak wrapped around her.

She had suffered so much already that she had come to believe herself calloused against further pain. But there were darker shadows than she had supposed.

Not until the news of the last battle had been brought to her, in Robert Forbes' house in the Cannongate, had she realized what love it was she had for the Glenallan. Previously there had been such swift motion and romance that her heart had been stunned. Excitement had drugged the hurt, as excitement in battle drugs the wounds that battle brings, and not until quiet had come did Lady Helen feel the full pain.

She sat for a long while in the dark, dirty room. All sorts of crazy notions slid through her brain. She might jump out of the window. Or quit the inn and walk straight toward those far hills from whence Malcolm had come, and walk and walk until she died. Or she might go to the place where he had fallen and die there. The old woman had said something about a river bank—she might drown herself.

One thing at least was certain: she would not go back to London. Gerald and her father, her mother too, would be genuinely pleased to learn that her husband had been killed. They would offer formal condolence, of course; but in their own minds they would think it a providential release from the results of an indiscretion. They did not know Malcolm. Nor did they know Lady Helen herself. They need not expect her back. She still breathed and could move; but this was false evidence. For all true purposes her life was ended now. Half a person cannot exist. Without a heart there can be no body.

Because of the shutters it was very dark in the room, and Lady Helen did not know whether night had come. She could hear, from where she sat, the faint whine of a breeze;

and beyond the shutters a small rain descended indifferently, irregularly.

There came a knock at the door. Lady Helen had begun to weep, but she wiped away the tears and opened the door. It was the hag. She entered quickly, a sideways, crablike movement, closing the door behind her. She went immediately to the window, peered through one of the largest cracks, and listened for a long time. Finally, satisfied, she turned to face Lady Helen, at whom she squinted suspiciously.

"Y'ken Callum MacIldowie?" she asked.

"He was my husband."

The hag shook her head. She did not believe that. The son of Douglas of Glenallan would never marry an English woman, she said bluntly.

Lady Helen showed her wedding ring, and explained:

"My grandmother was a Grant of Glenmoriston."

This information seemed to dispel much of the old woman's suspicion.

"Would that be Mary Grant, what went to Edinbro' an' married the German king's fellow—a gran' nobleman he was?"

"The Viscount Hornsby."

"Aye." The hag nodded thoughtfully. Grant blood—that changed it. She came closer, whispering. "Macdomhnull Dhu married you in Edinbro' town?"

"Yes. After they had taken the city. Before they marched across the border. Prince Charles himself attended the ceremony. Perhaps you—"

"Sh-sh! It's no' safe t' be speakin' the name o' Charlie in this place. The *siler roy* are everywhere."

And now Helen could bear this old woman's whispering no longer. She beat her hands together.

"Why do you ask me all this? You told me he was dead.

What more is there? What can I do now? Why did you come
here? Please get out!"

She threw herself on the bed, sobbing great sobs. The
hag, not at all offended, patted her shoulder.

"*Ochon*, lassie! It was in the street I tol' ye that. I did no'
dare say anything else there. I did no' ken ye were the wifey
o' Macdomhnull Dhu then."

Hope returned like a hard splash of light. Lady Helen sat
up.

"Is he safe? Tell me! Is he alive?"

But caution was the old woman's first policy. The bayonets of the Southrons were not easily forgotten. She pursed
her thin lips, stepping back from the bed.

"Sh-sh! There's a *siler roy* outside. They watch everywhere." She was at the door now. "Come after me. But do
no' step wi' me. No' till I turn."

And she was gone.

The street was deserted save for the hag when Helen quit
the inn. She followed the little hunched figure. She splashed
through puddles, and the mud stained her slippers and
showered in specks upon her cloak. It was necessary that she
walk fast, almost run, in order to keep the hag in sight.

There came a rumble of thunder—louder, louder, than a
great crash like the explosion of many cannons. A white flare
of lightning blinded her for an instant, and she stopped. But
the old woman ahead was rounding a street corner; and
Lady Helen wrapped her cloak closer about her and hurried
on.

At the edge of the town, where there was no candlelight,
the hag turned suddenly and waited for the tall lady to approach. And when Helen was beside her she drew from the
depths of her filthy dress a *skene dhu,* or Highland poniard

—triangular, single-edged, very sharp. She held it before her, point down. Helen did not move.

"Are you going to kill me?" Helen asked. The matter did not seem one of importance.

"Ye war no' lyin' t' me? 'Tis the truth ye're Callum Mac-Ildowie's wifey?"

"Why should I lie about that?"

"Maybe t' learn where he is, lassie. Maybe it's a Saxon spy ye be?"

Helen shook her head. She was no spy, she said. She was the wife of Sir Malcolm MacIldowie, the Laird of Glenallan, and she was proud of it.

The hag, clearly a woman of swift-changing moods, softened.

"An weel ye might be, lassie. There's no' a man bonnier in a' the world. Come along."

She refused to explain, but strode on along the narrow cart path across the moor, her feet splashing furiously in the mud, and her arms, bare to the elbow and horribly skinny, swinging at her sides as though they would propel her on her way.

Lady Helen followed obediently.

They were clear of the town now, and walking across part of the battleground. A few weeks earlier this land had been as wet with Scottish blood as today it was with rain. But it was very dark around them, and Lady Helen did not know whether they were going toward the river or toward the north hills. The thunder was almost constant now; and occasionally the lightning, by sheer brilliance, obliterated every object from sight.

They walked for a long time; it was impossible for Helen to know how long, or how far they had come. At last they arrived at a tiny native hut, a miserable structure, low and flimsy, more like a pigsty than a habitation for men. Here the old woman stopped. She motioned for Lady Helen to enter.

There was no lock. But at the first sound of Helen's hand on the door a sharp, low voice was heard:

"Who's there?"

She stood paralyzed. All this time she had not dared to hope, and now the relief overwhelmed her. She leaned against the doorway, unable for the instant to speak or move.

"Who is it? Speak up or you're dead!"

She rushed into the hut. She could see nothing. But she cried, again and again, the name of her husband.

"Malcolm! Malcolm!"

Her head struck the low ceiling. She bumped against a wall, moved her hands down the rough wood, found a blanket, a body—and fell into a deep embrace.

The world was restored to her. She had come up out of the grave. Malcolm's face was against her face, and Malcolm's arms were around her.

"God bless you, Eilidh! God bless you!"

There was a knock of flint, a spicking of thin tinder, the splutter of a candle in the middle of the hut, and then light. The Glenallan and his wife stared at each other, blinking.

He was frightfully thin and pale. His cheeks were sunk to hollows of white flesh, which an uncouth beard and the dubious flicker of the candle made to seem even more horrible. But his eyes glittered with the old spirit, and his chin protruded as arrogantly as ever. He was lying on a pile of straw, and covered with his own plaid, which was very dirty now and torn in several places. He had been holding pistols, but he had dropped these at the sound of his wife's voice.

She saw that his mouth was twisted back stiff as leather, and that his nostrils were squeezed tight. And she released him quickly.

"You're hurt! Oh, I've been hurting you!"

He almost smiled.

"You could not hurt me, Eilidh."

His voice was clear, calm, soft. There was the faintest film of moisture over his eyes, which might have been caused by the pain he felt or might have been caused by emotion.

"But you're wounded!"

"A wee cut in the shoulder. It will heal, now that you're here."

The old woman held up her candle, the better to view this pair. She was very pleased with herself. The innumerable wrinkles of her face splayed themselves into a vast grin of pride, and she clucked her tongue repeatedly against the roof of her mouth.

"You should have bandages!"

"Sh-sh! Do not be talking of it. They're only scars now, dried up and hard. Tell me what you've been doing and how you've been feeling and whatever brought you to this place. Lord, but it makes me strong to look upon you again!"

Smiling, he spoke to the hag:

"Aye, Jennie, it's my life you bring back to me first, and now it's my wife. If I was as rich as Argyll I could never be paying you for what you've done."

The old woman, like a fussy hen with chicks, bustled about the hut preparing her patient's supper. This was oatmeal mixed with whisky. Malcolm was delighted.

"Wherever did you get it, Jennie?"

"I stole it from Luckie Anderson's an' she's one can weel afford it, Macdomhnull Dhu, an' a' the *siler roy* buyin' at her place a' day an' a' nicht."

"You shouldn't steal, Jennie."

"Is it no' better I steal than you starve? It's Saxon money the slut's been takin'."

She set the dish before Malcolm, with a pewter spoon. To

him it seemed the rarest of delights. Lady Helen thought it raw and mean; but Malcolm assured her that there was only a choice now between oatmeal with whisky or oatmeal with water.

During the meal he explained. He had fallen by the banks of the Nairn while trying to cover Young Lochiel's escape. He could not remember much about the fighting, or did not care to tell her about it. Jennie—she seemed to have no other name—was one of the natives who had swarmed out over the moor when the pursuit had taken the redcoats away. Like the others, she had been looking for plunder. She had found Malcolm, and recognized the tartan. Her husband, one of the Glenallan clan, had been killed at Sheriffmuir while fighting under Sir Douglas MacIldowie, and Jennie believed that she still owed allegiance to all the descendants of the Black Donald. Forgetting thoughts of plunder, she had dragged this body away from the river bank and to her hut.

"She's wonderfully strong, Eilidh, though you wouldn't think it to look at her. She must have dragged me a mile, and me as good as dead then. I don't remember any of that part."

In the hut, after almost two days of nursing, she had revived him; and since that time she had been watching for his welfare, begging food or stealing it, or, whenever she had a chance, working for it.

"She'd be starving herself, if I let her," Malcolm whispered.

She had bandaged him, hunted herbs for him, and washed his wounds. There was a physician in Inverness, but Jennie and Malcolm had agreed that it would not be safe to send for him. She had guarded her secret well, and the Glenallan's survival was not known to any but these three. Time and again the Saxon soldiers had marched past the hut, but they thought it too mean to search. Malcolm had given his dirk to the kindly hag, but his pistols were with him always.

"They may get me yet, lassie, but I'll kill two of them first."

His wounds, Helen learned, were numerous, and at least one of them—the one in the left shoulder—was serious still. He could walk a few steps, leaning against the wall. But he was not strong enough to venture outside.

In town, Jennie talked little but listened much; and she kept her patient informed as well as any newsletter could have done. She told him about the butchery—about the Duke of Cumberland and General Hawley and their orgy of slaughter. She told him how, for weeks after the battle, the gallant clansmen had been hunted in every part of the land, and killed without mercy when cornered.

Jennie had told him, too, how Bonnie Prince Charlie rode like a madman to Simon Frazer's castle, and from there to the Clanranald's seat, and finally to the Islands of the West, where he skulked even now, in disguise, hunted by every available man of the English army and every available ship of the English navy. She had told of the Young Lochiel's escape to Lochaber, and of his concealment in a mountain hut with Cluny Macpherson of Cluny and the Young Macpherson. She had told him of the capture of Lord Lovat—that is to say, Simon Frazer—and of the Earl of Kilmarnock, and of Lord Balmerino, who before the uprising had been plain Arthur Elphinstone; and how Lord George Murray and the Duke of Perth and some others had escaped on a ship to France.

"*Ochon*, lassie! There's little the damned redcoats haven't done. But they've not caught the prince yet. He's on the mainland now, in Mackinnon country. When I get well I'm going to him, Eilidh. He'll be needing me."

"Haven't you done enough?"

He looked at her reproachfully.

"Not when he's in danger, Eilidh."

He was finished with the oatmeal, and he put the dish aside. He took her two hands again.

"All the time I've been away from you, Eilidh, I've been waiting for the day I'd be seeing you again, and the two of us happy and with no war. There's a sweetness in you, lassie, that takes the very breath away.

"But ye ken I can't be faithless to my fathers, Eilidh. My prince needs me. He's near the Glenallan country and the Cameron country. Can I sneak away to France, and him a penniless wanderer hiding behind trees in a land that should be giving him hospitality?"

He shook his head, sadly.

"Maybe he'll get safe away before I'm well and able to walk again. But if he doesn't, then I've got to go to him and help him."

CHAPTER 14

MALCOLM HAD CALLED IT JUST A wee cut in the shoulder. In fact it was a serious wound. For two days after Lady Helen's arrival he tossed with fever, muttering deliriously. Old Jennie guarded him with jealous eyes, administering herb extracts when she could induce him to take them, occasionally reciting incantations over him.

Helen wanted to send for a physician.

"It would be sendin' your lord t' the gallows," the crone cried.

Malcolm, too, objected.

"He'd only call the military, and I'm damned if I'll be their prisoner."

But it was a long hard struggle back to health. He had lost a prodigious amount of blood. The food that Jennie bought in the town, with Helen's money, helped to strengthen the patient; but it was all but a month before Malcolm was able to hobble about.

Meanwhile, no man ever received more loving care. With the rude miserable means at their disposal, Jennie and Lady Helen, the peasant and the heiress, did everything within their power to bring energy back to Malcolm. And all the while they watched for marauders. They never lighted a fire in daytime, for fear that the smoke would betray them; and at night they burned peat only after they had filled the cracks in the door and walls with wet earth to prevent the light from escaping. Helen rarely left the hut—only on foggy days or at night. Jennie went down to the town for food and whisky, but she avoided all talk with acquaintances.

This care Malcolm accepted from the old woman as a right. The common people of the Highlands always had served him. It was their duty, indeed their privilege, considering his birth. But that his wife should risk her health and wealth, her reputation, her very life—this astounded him. Accustomed to all London's comfort and all London's fashion, to be living in such a shack! She might return and be forgiven. The society in which she moved was not too prudish to permit this. Her father would accept a penitent; the marriage could be annulled; and there was her choice still of wealthy suitors.

Apparently she did not even think of this. And Malcolm was glad that his love had been well placed. For he would have loved her anyway. He could never have resisted her. That she had shown herself to be faithful as well as beautiful seemed to him a proof of divine generosity; and during the long nights while she slept beside him, with Jennie on the other side, he mumbled more than one prayer of thanks, though he was not, ordinarily, a praying man.

But obviously his duty was to his prince first.

"I'll go to Glen Allan. Fergus will know what's happened to Donald and Macpherson and the others. He'll know where Prince Charlie is, too."

Usually when he talked like this she nodded and smiled and said nothing. But once she asked him:

"Do you never think of taking me with you?"

The question shocked him. He started, staring at her.

"Take you! Why, lassie, do you ken what country I'll be going through? It's military everywhere. I'll spend every night outside."

"I would rather spend the night out-of-doors than in this smelly hovel."

Old Jennie, at the time, was outside cutting peat.

"But, lassie, there's all sorts of danger. The redcoats—"

"What do I care for the redcoats! I'm sick of hearing about redcoats! I'm not going to leave you again!"

"But—"

"I don't care how much danger there is. You've been through all the danger in the world and you're still alive. I won't let you go off again. If you go, I'll go with you."

For her, it was an extraordinary outburst. She had always been so amenable to his will, so quiet and complaisant.

But it did not annoy him. Rather it pleased him. He could not take the proposal seriously; it was not possible that this slim young bride of his could cross Scotland to the wild west coast. He shook his head, smiling, and to get her away from the subject he began to tell her about his ancestral home, concerning which she had more than once displayed curiosity.

"It's a braw country, Eilidh. But rough. There's many a deep stream, rushing along fast. And the hills are high, and the rocks are steep and sharp. But I know every path there is. I've hunted across every foot of it. There were many times I was lost in that London of yours, but I would never be lost in Lochaber.

"Where Allan's Castle is, it's the middle of a deep glen. That's Glen Allan. It was Malcolm Cleanmor, the great king that I was named after, who gave it to my ancestor, but the MacIldowies had really owned it long before that."

She smiled tenderly.

"You lived there all your life, Malcolm? You have no other estate?"

He was amazed at this question.

"Lord, lassie! Why should I be wanting another estate? There's no bonnier place in all the world than Allan's Castle. Maybe you'd think, at first, that it was gloomy. It's big and bare, ye ken. But when you get to live in it a while you get to love it, Eilidh."

He sighed.

"But it's Fergus'll rule there after this, Eilidh. I'll not see it but once again. But the clan won't die out. There are bairns in Glen Allan still, and they'll grow up and have children of their own. *Ochon!* There's never been so few of them, not at any time! The damned Campbells and the wars with the Southrons have done that. There was a time when the Glenallan could call out two hundred claymores—aye, and more, Eilidh, if the Campbells were coming. But the clan won't die out!" he boasted. "It could never die out!"

It pleased her to have him talk like this. For one thing, he was handsomest when he was describing something or somebody he loved. Enthusiasm sprayed a good light upon his somber countenance, and his eyes gleamed. And then, she never tired of observing the startling contrasts that his nature contained. With her, alone, he was loquacious and affectionate; elsewhere he was monosyllabic, haughty, cold. There were times when he was frugal, times when he was generous to extravagance. A stranger might think him cautious, hardheaded; yet Helen knew him to be a man of quick temper, who loved peril for its very own sake.

The whole business, now that she was with him again, seemed to take on the aspect of high adventure. Previously she had thought of the war with horror. Communication was bad, property was endangered, people were suspicious, the soldiers everywhere displayed an authority they never had in peace times; and worst of all, her husband might be killed. No good could come of it. Prince Charles, gay, gallant, picturesque, would be captured and hanged. The proud Highland chieftains, with all their finery and all their quaint customs, would be attainted, exiled, killed. It was a deplorable affair, and only tragedy could be expected to come out of it.

So she had thought, previously. But now that defeat had come, like a long-awaited guest, Lady Helen began to see that war as a brave, grand thing. She began to understand her husband's attitude. Tragic it was, but there was also about it something that was romantic. There would have been glory in victory; in defeat was poetry. The prince, so far away in hiding, had become even more fascinating than he had been when he led her through a minuet at Holyroodhouse.

She had plenty of time in which to allow this thought the freedom of her mind. Malcolm, though generally more talkative than she had ever before known him to be, was given also to long spells of moody silence; and she respected these spells by keeping to herself. She was bereft of the usual means of killing time. There were no theaters, no dinners, no novels to read or routs to attend. She could not ride; she could not even walk except at night, when walking was perilous in a country not familiar to her.

She realized now what a great portion of her time she had once spent at toilet. There was none of that in the hut. She worried about her looks.

Deprived of paint and powder and patches, she feared that her beauty was disappearing. She felt marred, smudgy.

Wet feet had given her a cold in the head, and her nose was runny and red. Her hair, unwashed these weeks, was dull, straight, lifeless. The freckles were reappearing on her face —more of them than had ever before been permitted to show themselves. All the stiffness had gone from her one dress, and what had been a charming simplicity, when she quit Inverness, was beginning to look like downright dowdiness. Jennie was vigorous with her needle, but not skillful. Every time Jennie mended a tear she somehow succeeded in detracting a little more from the original smartness of the one dress.

Malcolm, when Helen hinted her fears to him, shook his head indignantly.

"You are beautiful," he cried. "There isn't anybody in the world as beautiful as you."

"You say that because you want to console me."

He positively glared at her then.

"I say it because I ken what I'm talking about. Do I look blind? You might be dressed in the filthiest rags, lassie, and you'd still be fairer than any of them. You're beautiful *inside*, that's the reason."

Yet he himself was fussy about clothes. It was another facet of the man she was learning. All the sneers that she had heard him cast upon the fops of fashionable London were in her mind when she helped him to prepare his new kilt.

Among the things she had brought to the hut was the piece of Glenallan dress breacan Malcolm had given her before their marriage. She suggested that Jennie make a new kilt for him, since his own was badly ripped and patched. Malcolm at first protested that he would not take back a gift. Did she think he was a damned Lowlander? But later, when he could hobble about the hut, he agreed that a new kilt was a necessity.

And once the work was started, Helen helping whenever she was able, he began to display a nice taste in pleats. It must be just so. This way there was too much red showing, that way too much black. Now it was a finger too long, now half a finger too short. He became, for the four days that passed in the construction of this garment, a genuine nuisance. And when it was finally fitted on him—a process which itself he made into an elaborate rite—he wore it with the air of a man resigned to acceptance of a sloppy piece of work, a piece of work unworthy of his position.

Still, it made him feel good to be clad in new clean breacan. They patched his waistcoat and short coat as best they could, and he strapped the broad leather belts about him again, and hung the pistols in their places. The women could never know how much he missed the claymore, the genuine Andrea Ferrara. But it was a comfort at least to have the pistols and the dirk.

One night, very late, when Jennie was snoring, he said to his wife:

"I'm well now, Eilidh. I walked halfway to the town and back tonight, and I don't feel any pain. So—tomorrow I'm going back to the hills."

In the dark she felt for his hand, found it, squeezed it. The quiet announcement disarmed her. She had expected some formality about the departure. Malcolm was formal about every small thing, it seemed, but offhand about the great things.

"In the morning?" she asked.

"When the dawn comes up. Before the military are out snooping, lassie." He slid an arm under her neck and pressed his cheek to hers. "You—you'll be going back to London?"

"I'll be going along with you, Malcolm."

There was no outburst, no storm. Malcolm indeed said nothing at all for a minute or longer. Then he asked quietly:

"You're determined?"

"I am determined," she said.

He kissed her, there in the dark. It was a light kiss, rather a gay one, the sort a dandy might give. She could not see him, but she believed that he was smiling proudly, perhaps even grinning. Did he permit himself mirth when there was no light—this grave, punctilious husband of hers? She wondered. For all the intimacies of the hut, he was as much a mystery to her as ever he had been. She had expected an explosion—and he kissed her!

He said: "I love you." And then: "We must get sleep, lassie. No more talking. It's a hard trip. Jennie will wake us."

"Malcolm—"

"Sh-sh! We'll be needing the sleep. Good night to you."

"Good night, Malcolm."

CHAPTER 15

THREE WEEKS IT HAD TAKEN them to get to the edge of the Glenallan country, and it was persistent misery for Helen.

They had not always been able to travel. For four days and nights they had remained in the hut of a shepherd, who spoke no English, who treated Malcolm like a crowned king, and who wept when they went away. This was because of the nearness of some militiamen. Again, when redcoats were close at hand, they had crouched beneath an overhanging rock, half exposed to a steady monotonous drizzle, and surrounded by angry gnats, for a day and a night and a considerable part of the next day.

Malcolm tried to be sympathetic. Sometimes, when Helen was too tired to walk any farther, he would carry her for a few miles—carry her in his arms as easily as though she were a child. In spite of all the blood he had lost, he was much stronger than his wife, and every day the hills appeared to give him even more strength. He walked with long swinging strides. When they stopped at night, usually out of doors, it was Malcolm who scouted the countryside before he permitted a real rest; and it was Malcolm who dickered with what peasants they did meet, and who got what food they had, mostly oatmeal and brandy. He tried to be sympathetic —but he could not understand why she did not like oatmeal and brandy.

For three days before they came to the edge of the Glenallan country they had not spoken to anybody. There were more redcoats about, and Malcolm was especially careful. Sometimes they saw peasants or militiamen, but they remained in hiding as these fellows passed.

"I don't like their looks," was Malcolm's answer when Helen suggested, once, that they hail an apparently unarmed pair of mountaineers.

That was enough. Malcolm had seen the pair first; and he and Helen stayed behind some rocks until these men were well out of sight again.

"We're almost there now, aren't we?"

"We'll be at the end of the glen tomorrow morning." He was spreading tartan blankets on the ground. "When we see Fergus again it will be all right."

"You're very fond of your brother, Malcolm."

"Aye."

"Won't it be dangerous for him to entertain us at the castle?"

"We'll not stay at the castle. You will, aye. You'll get some rest and fresh clothes. But I'll stay away somewhere, so the soldiers can't have any excuse for arresting Fergus."

"Do you know of any place like that?"

"Aye."

He had been in high spirits, and had talked much about

what a bonnie lad Fergus was, and what a bonnie place was Allan's Castle. But as they neared Glenallan he became taciturn, grim. She knew him well enough to know that this meant he was excited. So she was silent.

In fact she was too tired to do much talking anyway. It had been a long hard day. Malcolm had walked faster than usual, and he had been less patient when she begged for rest. She sensed that even now he wanted to push on, and that if he had been alone he would have walked through the whole night to Allan's Castle. But she would not permit him to carry her again, for fear he might overstrain himself, and she could not walk another step of her own accord. So they had stopped.

Every night was like this. It seemed years since they had quit Jennie's hut near Inverness. Helen had no chance to think; she was too tired to think. Night after night she released her muscles like this, sinking upon a blanket spread over nothing softer than the bare earth—or, if they were lucky, some scrubby moss—and closing her eyes and aching all over until sleep rushed upon her like a wind.

So it was again this night. She remembered Malcolm, utterly silent, sitting near her, his back against a tree, eyes wide open—just sitting there, wrapped in his plaid, staring intently at nothing whatever. She called good night to him, and he smiled the tiniest bit, without turning his head. And the next thing she knew he was awakening her.

It was still dark under the trees, but through the mist she could see the faintest struggling streaks of dawn. She was still all one hot pain; but she knew that Malcolm was eager to be away.

"There's nothing wrong?" she asked.

He smiled, shaking his head, and he kissed her. But he said nothing at all. She knew that he was tremendously excited. What a lot his home meant to him! She watched him as he shook out her plaid and folded it and threw it over his shoulder. There was nothing for breakfast, and she knew this. He offered her the brandy bottle, almost empty; but she shook her head. She was thoroughly sick of brandy. So, still silent, he led the way across the bleak hillside.

The manner in which he moved among these hills had been a marvel to Helen from the first day. He told her that they were going far north to avoid the military, and he confessed that some of the countryside was strange to him, but yet he proceeded unerringly, as though his senses rather than his memory were leading him—as though he were a well-trained hunting dog on a good scent.

Now, so near to Glenallan, he moved faster than ever, his long legs carrying him across the broken, rocky hillside so rapidly that she was obliged, sometimes, to break into a nervous little trot in order to keep him in sight. She told herself, as she stumbled and staggered after him, that it could not last much longer.

Nor did it. Suddenly Malcolm broke into a run, and for a few minutes she could not see him at all, a circumstance that gave her a touch of panic. Then he reappeared on the brow of the hill not far away, his back to her. She ran toward him, and she came up behind him very quietly. He did not turn.

"This—this is the glen?"

"Aye."

It was a small glen, long, narrow. They stood on a hill near the middle of it, not far from the castle; but the ground mist still swirled below, and for a few minutes Helen could not distinguish that building clearly. She had, first of all, a sense of terrible desolation. Nothing moved in the glen. Not even a bird circled overhead. It was odd that she should feel this, for in the past three weeks she had seen very few human beings and no village or hamlet at all. She should

be accustomed to desolation. But at its very barest the
countryside through which she had been traveling had
seemed to conceal vitality, life, vibrancy; while Glen Allan
seemed to be absolutely dead.

Allan's Castle was a small brown building constructed of
rough stone—a square, ugly, strong edifice with two box-like
towers. Around it ran a narrow moat, dry, filled with rocks
and rubbish. One of its pair of iron gates was off its hinges
entirely; the other, unhinged on top, leaned away from its
companion. Behind was the loch, cold and perfectly clear,
across the surface of which the mist moved very slowly,
weirdly. The utter loneliness of the scene appalled her.
There was not a wisp of smoke, not a vine or flower.

Not far from the castle gates, and on the left of a little
mound there, she saw a group of square black masses. She
thought at first that these were clumps of black rocks, but
then, straining her eyes, she saw that they were ruined
houses, huts that had been burned to the ground.

She looked up at Malcolm. His mouth was drawn tight,
his eyes were staring wildly at the castle. She had never
seen him look so grim, so fierce. She was afraid of him again.

"You stay here," he said. "Keep back of those rocks."

"You'll be careful, Malcolm!"

"Aye. Stay here."

He pushed her gently behind the rocks. He unhooked the
pistols from his belt, examined the priming with his fingers,
but without looking at them, and cocked the weapons. He
had never taken his gaze from the castle.

Helen saw him stride down the hill. It was only a few
hundred yards to the castle gates. Once there had been a
drawbridge over the moat, but now there were only two
beams of iron without any planking between them.

Malcolm disappeared into the castle, swallowed up by
the tremendous shadows of the doorway.

On the hill, Helen waited for a long time, trembling. She knew that something horrible had happened, and she longed to go to her husband and try to comfort him, but she was afraid to move. But after a long while she came to be even more afraid of staying where she was. Wildly she feared that he might be dead, though no sound of any sort had come from the castle. He had walked so silently, in a manner so ghostlike, into that yawning black shadow—the blank emptiness of the place had engulfed him, removed him from the earth. Even though the mist had lifted, she could see no sign of Malcolm or anybody else at any of the narrow, fortress-like windows.

He had told her to remain on the hill; but she could no longer endure this. She rose, came from behind the rocks, and moved slowly, very slowly, down the hill. Sometimes she stumbled, for she did not look where she was walking and the ground was rocky and rough. She could not take her eyes from the square of blackness that was the castle doorway.

The drawbridge, she saw as she neared it, had been burned; the iron beams were twisted and blackened. The door itself had been burned too, or partially burned. What planks were left were blackened, splintered, and awry, forming no door at all. It required every bit of Helen's courage to pass through that doorway and into the blackness beyond.

At first she could see nothing at all, but she was instantly aware of a heavy, sickening stench. It was like walking into a tomb that had been stricken by lightning and forced to disgorge its grisly contents. So strong was this stink that for a moment she almost swooned. She swayed, gasping.

There were, she knew, stones all around her. The ceiling was low, the stone floor strewn with rubbish. Gradually her eyes became accustomed to the gloom, and she saw that she

was in a long blank corridor, a medieval sort of passageway
with no attempt at decoration. She could not see how it
ended; before her the darkness was complete.

She was standing there, wondering whether to go on,
wondering what to do, when a sound reached her that
chilled and stiffened the skin of her body. It was the faraway, muffled sound of a man sobbing. It rose and fell
softly, somewhere before her, somewhere in the recesses of
the castle.

It was Malcolm! She was convinced of it. She was convinced, too, that she must go to him and comfort him. She
started to run, not toward the door but away from it. She
stumbled and slid upon stones and empty bottles. She
bumped a wall, felt along it, found a doorway, entered that
to find herself in another passageway, somewhat lower and
lighter than the entrance corridor. Along this she ran, trying
to cry out—but she could not find her voice.

She paused at the end of this passageway, listening. The
sobbing was behind her now, and a little to the right. She
retraced her steps, running. She tried one door; it led to a
square room, utterly bare. She tried another door—and found
herself abruptly in the great hall of Allan's Castle.

It was a huge chamber, much bigger than Helen would
have supposed that the castle could contain. What furniture
it once held had been swept into the enormous fireplace at
the far end, where an attempt had been made to burn it.
Helen saw the stumps of chairs and stools, bits of what had
probably been a refectory table, charred chunks of an old
wall hanging, and a vast pile of old weapons. The fire must
have been a big one, for the walls all around the fireplace
were blackened. Above the fireplace, carved in the rough
stone, had been a crude escutcheon; but this had recently
been crushed and smashed, and bits of the stone were
strewn on the floor.

But what caught and held Helen's gaze was a group of dim, huddled figures on the floor to the left of the fireplace —grotesque, twisted, unmoving figures. And by the side of them, his face in his hands, knelt Malcolm MacIldowie of Glenallan, weeping like a woman.

She went to him, put a hand on his shoulder. He was not offended. He covered the thing at his side quickly with a remnant of tartan blanket; but she had seen it. She had seen other, similar things around it. In that dim light and from the other side of the chamber they had not looked so horrible; but now, close to them, she was sick. Malcolm rose quietly, put an arm around her and, without a word of reproach, led her back through the two corridors and to the doorway. It was wonderful to breathe clean air again.

"Go back where you were, Eilidh. I'll come to you soon. I must put him away decently first."

"Was it—was—"

"It was bonnie Fergus," he said very quietly. "They did it with their bayonets. They must have made up some excuse. Or else they were just drunk. Now, go back there. I'll come soon."

She walked away without another word, and Malcolm returned to the castle. From the hillside, Helen watched him carry out his brother's corpse—watched him dig a pitifully shallow grave by the edge of the loch, using the only available tool, his dirk—watched him bury what had been Fergus MacIldowie Macdomhnull Dhu of Glenallan. He was steady about it, well contained, methodical. He did not look around him, and he wasted no time. When the job was finished he did not even pause for a last look at the miserable little pile, but wiped his dirk and replaced it in its sheath, and then came directly to her on the hill.

"Let's get away from here."

"Was there—was there nobody left, Malcolm?"

"Nobody," said Malcolm. "Let's get away."

He did not turn his head as they quit the place, but Helen could not resist peeking over her shoulder. Glen Allan was utterly still, desolate, like a valley on the moon, silent, life-less. Not even a dog prowled among the ruins of the huts. Not even a bird circled overhead.

CHAPTER 16

FOR MANY HOURS AFTER THAT they walked in silence. Helen wanted to speak to him, but she did not know what to say, and she feared that he would resent any attempt to comfort him. He walked with his head down, but he was watchful; he walked slowly. And when twilight was coming, and they were at one end of a narrow glen, about to start over a wooded rise of ground, he stopped dead, like a fairy story character who had been turned to stone.

Helen could hear no sound, and she could see nothing more alarming than the long gray shadows, lilac in the hol-low places, that were beginning to stretch themselves across the hillsides, and the trees and heather and rocks.

Perhaps Malcolm could see nothing either. But he sensed something.

"What is it?" she whispered.

He shook his head, but did not answer. For a little time his dark eyes darted back and forth; he was searching the shadows, which were perfectly still. Then slowly he un-hooked the pistols from his belt, and held them, one in each hand, and cocked them with his thumbs. He walked slowly backward, motioning her back with an elbow, but never turning his head, never taking his gaze from that shadow-mottled hillside.

At a tree they paused, and he pushed her behind it. There

he waited, pistols ready. And she too waited, with a wildly beating heart.

For perhaps two minutes nothing whatever happened. Then from the shadows came a voice—a harsh voice—calling some challenge in Gaelic.

"I do no' ken ye while ye're hid," Malcolm replied calmly. "Stand up, if ye be no coward."

There was a murmur of talk, and not one but four men rose from their places of concealment. They had been hiding behind some rocks and heather, startlingly close at hand.

Each had a musket, pointed at Malcolm.

"I wish to look at ye," Malcolm called.

He walked, all undismayed, directly toward the four muskets. A show of utter fearlessness was his best protection at the moment, and he knew it. If he displayed any fight, they would shoot him down.

He came close to the first man, the man who had spoken —a monstrously tall fellow dressed in the Highland kilt and philibeg, with a red bonnet and rough brogues, but no stockings; he carried, in addition to the musket, a pistol, a broadsword, and three or four knives. His black hair hung thick and matted around his shoulders, and his black beard tumbled down over a huge, deep chest.

Malcolm stared at him for some time through the gathering gloom. The two men were only a few feet apart.

Then Malcolm said: "You are Patrick Grant."

The man did not answer.

"They call you Black Peter of Caskie," Malcolm went on. "I have been looking for you."

"Ye've found me," said the giant.

He did not stir.

"I want you to tell me where a certain person is hiding."

"It's a lot to ask. There's no reason why I should no' kill ye an' be done wi' it."

Malcolm frowned impatiently.

"Looney! Do ye no' ken it's the Glenallan who talks?"

The big fellow started. He peered forward to get a closer look: he put his face almost against Malcolm's face, staring suspiciously. Then he became obsequious.

"Forgive me, Macdomhnull Dhu. I did no' ken it was you."

They had been speaking in Gaelic, and Lady Helen, crouching behind her tree, did not understand it. Now Malcolm returned to her, hooking his pistols to his belt again. The four men had lowered their muskets.

"These are loyal," Malcolm told his wife. "I heard of them through Jennie. They are called the Seven Men of Glenmoriston, and they don't mean to submit to the redcoats. They don't consider the war finished yet, and they're still fighting it—in their own fashion."

"They are—outlaws?"

"Aye." Malcolm smiled grimly. "Outside of the prince himself, there's nobody Hawley would rather catch than this Black Peter. But he'll tell us where the prince is hidden. We'll go with them."

"But if—"

"You forget my blood," he said coldly. "Besides, I'll tell them that your grandmother was a Grant of Glenmoriston."

"They might think you're lying."

"Would a MacIldowie lie?"

They followed Patrick Grant and his companions for about a mile, striking off over a hill to the left.

It was utterly dark, and raining a little, when they came to the mouth of the cave. A tiny opening it was, and Lady Helen would never have suspected, even if she had seen it in the daytime, that it led to any place of habitation. It seemed no more than a crack in the rocks, half hidden by the heather that was thick about it.

Somebody called a low challenge as they approached, but

Patrick Grant only grunted in response. They could not see the challenger, but soon something behind the rocks was moved and a dim light showed through.

"If the lady will get down on her knees—"

She hesitated, looking at Malcolm. But he nodded reassuringly.

"Go in, Eilidh. I'll follow you."

She crept through the tiny opening. She had to kneel very low, and before she reached the cave proper she had to get down on her stomach and crawl for a few feet.

Then the narrow tunnel widened abruptly, and she found herself in a large, low chamber of rock lit by a bogpine torch that flickered weirdly at the other end. Directly through the center of this chamber flowed a clear, cold stream of water. The torch was thrust into a crack in the rock wall, and the only furniture was a three-legged stool. There was a heap of blankets in one corner, and everywhere there were weapons—many claymores, cavalry sabers, muskets, knives.

Three men were squatting under the torch. They rose when she entered, and stared foolishly at her, blinking as though they could not believe their eyes. They did not speak. But when Malcolm came out of the tunnel and got to his feet, standing as straight as the low ceiling would permit, one of those men gave a cry of recognition.

"Do ye no' ken me, Macdomhnull Dhu?"

"Aye," said Malcolm. "You're a Lochaber man from the other side of Lochiel, but I disremember your name."

Thereafter he spoke only to Lady Helen and to Patrick Grant, and his manner in treating with the leader of the band was cold, haughty. Yet all of these men, like the other commoners they had encountered in their trip across the hills, treated him with an extravagant awe.

He had no money, no followers or servants, no official

position. He was an outcast, wanted by the beaks. But—he was a descendant of Donald the Black.

They washed in the stream, which was very cold, and dried themselves before a fire one of the men kindled on the rock floor. There must have been an opening of some sort in the back of the cave, for there was a continuous, chilly draft, and most of the smoke was carried out promptly through the entrance tunnel. The outlaws did not approach the fire until Malcolm and his bride had dried themselves thoroughly. Then they served minced collops with butter, oatmeal with brandy, and some main bread. Patrick Grant apologized for the meal, the best they'd had in a month. If he had known they were coming, he protested, he would have arranged for venison and partridge and shortbread. But he was pleased to be able to offer them some good wine.

The wine, muscatel and sack, was more than just good—it was astounding. The muscatel was the best Lady Helen ever had tasted. Sick of brandy and whisky, neither of which she had ever liked, she was delighted. The wine warmed her more than the fire did, and it made her sleepy.

"Where do you suppose they got it?" she whispered.

Malcolm grinned.

"Where they get everything else they need. The German's officers," he explained, "like to live well, even out here in the wilderness."

"But how could they buy wine from such men?"

"They don't buy it."

"You mean they *steal* it?"

She was whispering still. The cave made whispering natural, for a raised voice set millions of eerie echoes into motion.

"They just go and take it," Malcolm explained.

"But they can't attack regular army forces!"

"If half of what I hear about them is true, these fellows

can attack anything. When Charles was here they had champagne for him."

"The prince was *here?*"

"Stayed here three weeks. These men worship him."

She looked around the dim strange place, looked at the bare walls over which the yellow flight flickered erratically, and across the rough bare floor.

"An odd place for a prince," she commented.

"He's been in many a worse since that fight on Drummossie Muir."

"Is he near here now?"

"That's what I'm about to ask."

For some time, then, Malcolm talked in a low voice, in Gaelic, with Patrick Grant. Helen was nodding, drowsy, when he returned to her.

"We'll stay here the night. In the morning I'm going out to join His Highness. He isn't far from here, but I can't take you to the place. Patrick Grant will get some horses in case His Highness needs them, and in the morning he'll take you to a hut near here where there's a woman named Maisie. Maisie will take good care of you, and I'll come to you in a few days—maybe with the prince and maybe without him."

She was frightened again, and clung to him; she was no longer sleepy.

"I don't want you to go away without me!"

He put an arm about her and spoke gently, reassuringly.

"No harm will happen to either of us, lassie. It's the only thing we can do. A French ship's coming to Lochnanaugh, and we must be with the prince when he escapes. We'll go to France with him and he'll get me a commission in the French army. MacIldowies," he added solemnly, "have fought for France in the past."

"But in this wild place—"

"Hush, lassie. Do you suppose I'd leave you if I thought

any harm could come to you? Patrick Grant has kissed his dirk and sworn to protect you with his life, and a Glenallan lady is always safe with old Maisie."

"But why can't you go with me?"

He shook his head.

"I must go to the prince."

There was no arguing with Malcolm; she knew that. But for all the physical weariness she felt, she lay for many hours, tossing in a tartan blanket, before she could get any sleep that night. As she was stretching out, she saw two of the men quit the cave, after Patrick Grant had spoken to them. They were going to get some horses, Malcolm told her. There was a company of dragoons stationed nearby.

His Royal Highness, Charles Edward Louis Philip Casimer Stuart, Prince Regent of England, Scotland and Ireland, Prince of Wales, Count of Albany, Baron of Renfrew, etc., etc., sat in the back of the Cage, one hand indolently turning over and over a fish that was frying, while the other hand held a mug of claret. He had been drinking for two days, and neither hand was steady.

At the table, bending low to spare their heads the scrape of the ceiling, were Cluny Macpherson of Cluny, Macpherson the Younger of Breakachie, the Reverend John Cameron, and a helot named Sandy. They were playing cards. Thirty-two guineas in silver were on the table; it was all the money that was left. From time to time it was distributed evenly again and the game restarted.

Malcolm sat with Donald of Lochiel at the doorway, gazing across a sweep of blackness that was fronted by a few vaguely looming pine trees and overhung with ten thousand silver pinpricks in a black sky. The smoke wandered lazily, teasingly past their faces, and the smell of fish was welcome. They had not eaten cooked food for two days, for until this night it had been deemed unsafe to light a fire in the Cage.

The Cage was a simple but effective place of refuge. Half cave and half house, originally it had been no more than a sizable hole in the side of a cliff, some twenty feet above the ground. A series of steps, some natural, some chipped into the rock, led up to it. The doorway was so cleverly constructed of tree branches and foliage indigenous to the cliffside itself, that only a man who was very close to it, or a man who on a clear day was in search of just such a place, would be likely to observe it.

Donald and his cousin were fighting Culloden over again.

"And if only the Macdonalds had charged—"

"Nay, it would have done no good, Callum. It would have been that many more brave laddies killed."

"*We* broke through!"

"How many of us?" Lochiel asked. "Nay, we were beaten before the battle started."

Malcolm shook his head.

"Maybe you're right. Those damned Englishmen—"

Charles Edward interrupted, drawling:

"Glenallan, you're the most perfervid English hater I have ever encountered. Tell me, why do you carry that old feeling so persistently? Can't you find anything good to say about Englishmen at all?"

Malcolm considered respectfully. Young Lochiel and the prince waited, smiling. The prince turned the fish over again, causing a great splutter in the pan and a shower of tiny hot sparks.

"Nothing," Malcolm said at last.

And now Lochiel and the prince both laughed aloud, so that the whist players looked up from their game. Charles Edward swallowed the last of the wine and explained for their edification.

"Our gallant Glenallan has been denouncing the English again. He can think of nothing good to say about them—nothing at all." His highness addressed himself to Malcolm, squinting through the smoke. "But surely you must concede that there were men of courage on the other side at Falkirk and Culloden? Surely they were not *all* base?"

"Practically all," said Malcolm.

This was a subject that excited the strongest feelings in him; and just now he was additionally irritated by the patronizing manner of the others.

"You don't understand," he cried. "I don't hate them just because they are English. I hate them—"

He paused, embarrassed. He rose to his feet, but after bumping his head against the rock sat down again. The prince made some courteous remark. The others only smiled.

"You don't understand. I hate Saxons because they want to make the world just like themselves. I hate them because they think everything they do is right, and that God in Heaven gave them special commands to do it just that way."

Words were coming easier now, though he was not saying one tenth of what he meant.

"We must all talk English. We must forget the Gaelic. Gaelic is wrong because Englishmen don't understand it. We must give up the kilt because Englishmen don't wear kilts. So—wearing a kilt is indecent. We must not own muskets or pistols. We might shoot Englishmen with them. But we must not even shoot one another, because Englishmen don't approve of that.

"They come to Scotland and say so. The Lowlanders listen—and obey. That's because the English have money, and the Lowlanders are like the English—they want money, and anything that prevents them from getting it they call treasonous or mad or anything they feel like calling it, and they demand that it be abolished. And the Lowlanders listen to that and imitate them. Pass the bottle."

He felt like striding back and forth, swinging his arms. But he remembered the ceiling. The claret wetted his mouth and felt good in his throat.

"It's more. The Saxons and all the others like them are killing everything I love. And they aren't even killing it out in the open. They just call it uncivilized, and clink their moneybags, and act high-and-mighty—and those cursed Lowlanders bow to them and agree.

"They're *sensible*, that's it!" The English, I mean. The Lowlanders, too. Everything they do must be *sensible*. To hear them talk you might think that everybody who wasn't sensible was a loon or a knave."

The Stuart offered: "But surely, Glenallan, common sense is an excellent thing? I have even observed you to use it yourself on occasion."

"Oh, on occasion, aye. But has Your Highness ever seen me forcing it upon somebody else? Have you ever seen me retreat to common sense when honor told me to move forward? No! And you have never done so yourself, Sire. Was it common sense to meet them at Culloden when we were so weak we could hardly hoist our swords? Yet Scots will remember that day as long as there are Scots. Even the Lowlanders, after they have counted their money for the night, and sneaked off to whimper their prayers to a Presbyterian God—they'll wish that they could have done that themselves.

"Sire, was it sensible to march over the border with a few thousand men, and half of them with no guns and half of them barefooted? To march into England where trained troops were waiting for us, a dozen to one? For the matter of that, Sire, was it sensible to start this business in the first place?"

"It was *right!*" Charles Edward himself was excited now.

"I came to take back what had been stolen from me and my family. It was the right thing to do."

"Aye," said Malcolm, cooler now, "and that's why we did it. Look at Lochiel here. He's been smiling at me, thinking how daft I am and pretending to be calm and hardheaded himself. But didn't he know when he summoned his clansmen—didn't he know that the chances were he'd get only poverty and death for reward? A year ago he was rich, and the most respected laird benorth of Tweed. What is he now? He's sneaking around the countryside, ducking behind a tree every time he hears a twig snap, without any money, without any servants—and him who used to mount a tail of thirty-odd gentlemen! His castle burned to the ground, and all his land taken from him. . . . Yet he knew when he summoned his clan that the chances were ten to one against him." Malcolm faced his cousin. "You did, Donald. Admit it."

"Aye," said the Young Lochiel. "I knew that."

Malcolm waggled both hands, triumphantly gesturing. John Cameron and the Macphersons nodded. Only Sandy was astonished. The confidence that Lochiel had seemed to possess during the campaign—a confidence affected for the purpose of encouraging his warriors—had appeared genuine to Sandy, who never dreamt of doubting his chief.

Malcolm indicated the Macphersons, father and son.

"Did Cluny think he was going to come out alive when he pledged his clan to Your Highness's service? But it was the *right* thing to do, it was the *honorable* thing. So he walked into the war at the head of all his men, though he might have hung back and dickered for terms like Lovat, or refused outright, like the Macdonald of the Isles, damn his black soul! Was that sensible, what Cluny did?"

The Macpherson nodded, while his son smiled. Charles Edward was looking curiously at them.

The Macpherson said: "I didn't believe, any more than Lochiel, that our arms would be victorious. But what else could I do? I couldn't disobey my king."

"The Campbells could," Malcolm cried. "And the Lowlanders! And the Saxons!"

But now Charles raised his hand.

"The gallant Glenallan," he said, "is surely to be listened to with respect when he speaks of honor, for he knows what honor is. But he must permit me to insist that he's unjust when he condemns all Lowlanders and all Englishmen. You must remember, Sir Malcolm, that there were Lowlanders under our banner at Falkirk and at Culloden—yes, and at Gladsmuir too. They had left their homes. They had risked disgrace and death. And they had no hills to retreat to, remember that. The hired soldiers of the usurper—"

Sandy interrupted: "If Your Highness please, sir, the fish is burning."

Prince Charles laughed, and took the pan from the fire.

"I hope I'll be a better king than I've been a cook," he said. "Do you remember Alfred and the cakes?"

In fact, he was an excellent cook—better even than Sandy, who had been in Lochiel's kitchen for many a year. He frequently elected to prepare their meals, hot or cold, and took no small pride in his own ability. The fish, despite the burning, was a pleasant food, hot and savory. It was placed on a wooden trencher in the middle of the stone table, and they used their fingers for eating it, the Stuart himself dividing it equally among them.

After claret had washed this down, they returned to the conversation. Donald of Lochiel had his say.

"I think my cousin is right in many particulars, but I must agree with Your Highness that he has condemned Englishmen too sweepingly. The war was not really that. If Your Highness will permit me to say it, I believe it was a war between those who were convinced that the rightful king should sit on the throne and those who were convinced that farmers and merchants should make laws for gentlemen to obey. Perhaps the merchants are right. I don't think so."

"I can not jibe entirely with either of you," said Prince Charles. "No. Since we are being frank tonight, it was not a war of Highlanders against the rest of the world—nor was it a war of those who had faith in my family against those who dreaded to lose their new advantages. It was rather a war against a religion.

"Those soldiers under the German's banner were not fighting me. They were fighting the Holy Father in Rome"—he crossed himself—"and they believed that His Holiness would dominate their lives and their politics if my father became the real king. No arguments, no written contracts or solemn vows, could make them think otherwise. They were blind in their hatred of the Romish church—believe me, gentlemen—and that was the reason they opposed us, and it was the only reason.

"I can't understand it! They call us of the church bigoted! They tell their neighbors, and their neighbors echo that nonsense. They cry that we would overpower the country and kill all other beliefs and burn all other churches, and that His Holiness would encourage this outrage and direct it."

There were tears in his eyes, and he struck his knees vigorously.

"I can't understand it! If you gentlemen could only meet the Holy Father. . . . He is amiable and gracious and so sweet in everything he does. But they paint him as a monster—they who have never even seen him.

"This was never properly a matter of religion. What does it matter what I believe, or what my father believes? It is the same God, isn't it? Why do men scream that their own way of worshiping is the only right way?"

"Because they are Englishmen," said Malcolm.

Charles Edward smiled, but it was a sad smile.

"No, Glenallan. For I have found that horrid spirit every-where. But I cannot see what difference the belief makes in a king. If he is a good man and of good blood he will be a good king, Catholic or Protestant. If he be a bad man, basely born, then he will be a bad king, even though every sub-ject in his land agrees with his churchly opinions. And yet, that was the principal cause of the war."

But Sandy and the Reverand Mr. Cameron had fallen asleep, their snores growling large out of small preliminary wheezes. All of these men had to get up at dawn, for they had learned that the French ship really was waiting for Prince Charles at Lochnanaugh and they were to travel the following day to the hut where Lady Glenallan was waiting.

So, when the claret and the fish were finished, his royal highness stretched himself upon the pile of peat that was to be his bed, wrapped himself in a dusty torn blanket, and resigned himself to slumber.

The Macpherson crawled under the table and lay down by the side of his son. Wrapped in a breacan, they too were soon asleep.

And Donald and Malcolm, left alone, sat by the entrance of the Cage, talking quietly of this and that, while the easy night breeze fanned their faces, bringing an odor of pine needles.

It was good to be with Donald again. It made Malcolm feel quieter, calmer. It was good, too, to know that Prince Charles at last was virtually safe, after these many months of skulking, and that he and his bride would soon be on a vessel bound for another land, away from all the fuss and fighting.

They sat there until dawn, when they awakened the others.

CHAPTER 17

HELEN RAN DOWN THE HILL and went directly to him, and took his hands.

"I was so frightened, Malcolm!"

He shook his head, smiling. In an undertone he chided her for having spoken to him before she curtsied to the Prince of Wales. She was apologetic, for she knew what importance he attached to these trifles.

"But how much longer must it be?"

"A very wee time. Cluny Macpherson and Donald and the others are going on now to Lochnanaugh where a ship's come to take us all away. His Highness and you and I will stay here tonight while the rest go ahead." He glanced toward the hut. "Has Maisie watched you well, lassie?"

"Oh, she's been wonderfully kind. She made me stay inside while she did all the work and all the watching."

The Stuart spoke.

"Gentlemen, shall we not have a dram together before you continue your journey? I observe that there are horses here, and we who remain will have an easier trip of it perhaps."

Maisie scurried back into the hut, to emerge a moment later with two bottles of whisky. There were no glasses. They drank to King James, to the captain of the waiting ship, and finally, at the suggestion of King James's son, to Lady Glenallan: "The bravest wife ever a Scottish laird had. . . ."

Then the other strode off down the hill and away, and the four who remained retired to the hut. The Stuart, confident that his troubles were soon to be ended, was in high spirits and insisted upon chatting. He drank throughout this conversation; but in the afternoon, made thoughtful by the whisky, he lapsed into silence, giving Malcolm and his bride an opportunity for their own exchanges.

Soon it was night. A partition divided the hut into two tiny rooms, and Maisie and Helen retired to the inner one, sharing a single bed in spite of the old woman's embarrassed protest. Charles, who had refused to take the bed at the expense of a lady, made himself comfortable on a pile of straw in the outer room, near the wall. And Malcolm slept on some peat at the doorway, a musket and two pistols by his side.

"Are you comfortable there, Glenallan?"

"As snug as I would be in a featherbed, Highness."

"But there's no need now for such precaution. Come over with me. We'll keep one another warm. And I have plenty of room here."

"If Your Highness please, it's safest to watch the door."

In the darkness Charles Edward shook his head. Before this he had found occasion to marvel at the intensity of this young man's devotion. To loyalty he was accustomed. Obedience he accepted as his natural right. But the devotion of Sir Malcolm of Glenallan, instead of flattering him, sometimes almost irritated him.

For Glenallan was fighting and starving, and risking the life and the honor of his bride and himself, for something more than a prince of the blood royal, as Charles perceived. There was more to his loyalty than the feeling of duty that a faithful subject should have, some ideal that was beyond and above the Stuart ideal—some awful force of egotism, perhaps, that made this young man stretch himself to heights of sacrifice that were scarcely human.

"I wonder," Charles Edward muttered to himself as he lay there in the darkness. "I wonder whether these men think that their families are nobler than mine? I wonder whether it isn't really their own ancestors who are leading them through all this fury?"

He never could understand these tall, dour chieftains. They were a race apart, so different from the French and Italians, different too from the English. Behind their grave, dark faces there must have been strange throughts; inside their hearts they must harbor curious emotions.

All were up at daybreak. They had whisky and oatbread for breakfast. Maisie got permission to go out in search of berries, and soon she was lost from sight in the woods at the foot of the hill. Malcolm tended the horses—at least until Prince Charles, impatient with his clumsiness, took the task from him and finished it properly.

"You were never made for a groom," the prince said.

"I hope not, Sire."

Lady Helen watched with a smile. She often wished that her husband knew more about horseflesh and could ride better. She could not be rid of the old conviction that he is not a perfect gentleman who is not a perfect horseman; and one of the things she most admired about the Stuart was his seat in saddle.

They left the animals tethered before the hut, while Charles Edward and the Glenallan retired to the inner room to discuss, over a bottle, the question of whether it would be wiser to start for Lochnanaugh immediately or wait until night.

Helen sat in the doorway, watching for the return of Maisie. It was one of those days that are rare in the Scottish Highlands—sunny, warm, almost enervating. Though the night was scarcely gone, there was not a trace of mist on the hilltops, and the sky was clear and blue without clouds.

The sun made her think of France. Would she be in France soon? Or would this mad adventure end in death? Would the prince yet be taken? She shuddered to think of what Malcolm might do if this happened. Malcolm would become a maniac. Sometimes, Helen reflected, Malcolm's spirit held just a hint of the ludicrous, like an old legend that everybody loves but nobody any longer believes; but always it was admirable, and often it was magnificent.

And the thing that made one marvel, suppressing superior smiles that came too quickly, was the realization that, after all, he was a crack shot, an expert swordsman, a seasoned soldier, and a wise and prudent leader of men. For all his high-flown ideas, for all his old-fashioned chivalry, he could fight with the best of them, and he could think in an emergency, and act. Indeed, he seemed to think clearest and act best in moments of peril.

A red deer emerged from the bushes that surrounded the clearing below, gazed at her a moment, then deliberately browsed, inching away. The sun rose slowly, reaching its fullness like a giant stretching.

Her dress needed mending again. For all the care she lavished on it whenever she had a chance, this poor dress was forever getting torn. Her needle was in the back room. She rose with a sigh, for she felt uncommonly lazy there in the sunlight. She interrupted the two men, murmuring apologies.

"I only wanted this . . . Do sit down, Your Highness. Positively, sir, you embarrass me with so much attention."

It was on her way back to her stool in the doorway that she stopped, suddenly wide awake. Her eyes flushed with terror and grew very big; the needle and thread fell from her hand.

The ground that sloped away before the hut was bare of trees and high bushes for several hundred yards, a precaution. At the foot of the hill was a small clearing, broad but not deep, and beyond this was a shady wood. Rocks were few here, and the heather was not thick.

The Lady of Glenallan saw a tall broad-shouldered man in scarlet and blue riding out of the wood. At his side clanked a heavy cavalry saber; his boots were bright in the sun; there was gold lace on his hat, gold froggery across his chest. Immediately behind him came two other men, one on each side of the first figure; and behind them, riding in perfect order, with their carbines in the hollows of their right arms, were some twenty-five or thirty dragoons.

The leader seemed startled at the sight of the hut. He reined hastily. He signaled to the others, and they all retreated into the wood like men who do not wish to be seen. Afterward, the peaceful sunshine beat upon that spot as though no human being ever had been near.

CHAPTER 18

THE OLD WOMAN's death was annoying. And Fitzstephen was the more angry because he had only himself to blame for it: it was he, as captain, who had ordered the soldiers to twist that arm a little harder and to keep twisting until the damned old witch told them what they wanted to learn. But how was he to know she was so feeble? To look at her, a man would think her as tough as any of these damned barbarians.

Now, with her gone, they were obliged to find the hut on her scant information. At the top of a hill, she had gasped, with a cleared space before it, bog on either side . . . It was in this direction, roughly.

They rode slowly, Fitzstephen in the lead. And quite without warning he found himself in a clearing, a quiet spot saturated with sunlight, at the foot of a hill upon which there was a hut. There were two fine horses tethered to a post before that hut. Both were saddled.

Lieutenant Button and Lieutenant Harris had followed

Fitzstephen out of the wood, one on either side. The captain wheeled about.

"This is the place! That's it! Get back!"

Behind the protecting barrier of trees, they gazed with more care and laid plans for a cautious approach. The hill and hut were perfectly still. Was the Young Pretender resigned to surrender? It did not seem probable. More likely, Fitzstephen told his fellow officers, some Highlanders were waiting up there with muskets and swords and clubs, prepared to make one last desperate stand.

If this were indeed the case, they could shoot three or four men with ease before the hut was taken. There was no way to approach it under cover. On right and left were swampy grounds. To send a squad around to the rear would take too much time. Besides, they did not know how many men might be in that hut; and if they split their force they might be surprised by a sally. Presumably, these fellows would be bold enough to try anything; they all knew that the gallows awaited them.

Still, there was nothing at all to indicate that the hut was occupied—nothing except those horses. They were good horses, and they looked somehow familiar to Captain Fitzstephen.

The door was open, but they could not see beyond that, for the hut had no window.

The captain cursed the old woman again. It had been a piece of excellent luck, capturing her and forcing the secret from her. But she might have stayed alive long enough to guide them here and give them further details, so that they could advance with more discretion. As it was, how did they know that they had not been seen? How did they know that the hillside, when they started up, would not become white with smoke from a dozen guns?

Captain Fitzstephen spoke suddenly, interrupting Button's suggestion that they hoist a white flag for parley.

"We've been here too long already. The hag said there was only one man guarding him. The only thing to do is ride straight up the hill. You gentlemen will ride with me. All the men must follow close."

Harris suggested: "Why not dismount and walk it? Then we could at least crouch down."

"Yes," said Button. "Then we'd not be such good targets."

Fitzstephen shook his head.

"Suppose they make a dash for it? We'd be obliged to run back here and mount again before we started after them. And those horses look fast."

So the full troop started forward—none too rapidly at first, for the men were not eager to rush into a volley fired by an invisible enemy. Fitzstephen rattled his saber and turned in his saddle, urging them to hurry. Harris grabbed his shoulder.

"*Look!*"

Two figures had rushed out of the hut. One was in native Highland garb, with a sword at his side and pistols on his belt. The other wore a tattered blue coat still rich with lace, and a yellow waistcoat, yellow breeches. The Highlander was tall and dark; the other was almost equally tall, but of light complexion, and strikingly handsome. On the breast of the second gleamed a bright Star of St. Andrew, the royal order of Scotland.

Fitzstephen shouted, half for joy, half in alarm.

"Get them! Get that first fellow! *I want him alive!*"

The one with the decoration had mounted the farther horse. With one graceful leap he was in saddle, and he wheeled. The Highlander, standing between his companion and the oncoming dragoons, fired one of his pistols directly at them. Then he too mounted, though clumsily; and both of them disappeared behind the hut.

The captain drew his saber as he rode, flourishing it over his head. He shouted at the top of his lungs: "I want them *alive!*"

The ground behind the hut, unlike the ground before, was rocky. The dragoons from the beginning had a hard time of it. One of them already had been pistoled by the Highlander. Two others were thrown when their mounts stepped into holes. But there were plenty left. They leaned forward, riding without regard for order or discipline, the best mounted and the boldest drawing ahead, the others falling back.

The first fugitive, very straight in the saddle and riding like a master, could be seen only intermittently between the leaves of the low-boughed trees. The other, the Highlandman, was nearer. The Highlandman was having trouble with his horse, and ne rode awkwardly; but there was a pistol in his right hand, and he was obviously determined to do what he could to delay the pursuit.

They jumped a stream where the water was thrown high into the air when it hit the heavy stones and was broken into the finest rainbow spray. They crossed a clearing, frightening a doe. They rounded a pile of gaunt brown rocks grouped fantastically. They started on another upgrade.

The pursuers were drawing out. Their captain, riding well ahead, still flourished his saber, but he had ceased to shout. A sergeant, a fellow named Peterson, was fully three lengths behind him, and after Peterson came Lieutenant Button and three others, while Harris and the rest of the company were strung along in the rear.

Fitzstephen had almost drawn alongside of the Highlander when the captain's horse stumbled and fell. Fitzstephen rolled off easily, sprang to his feet, and mounted again, the horse rising quickly from a mere bed of moss. It was done in two blinks of an eye. But it gave Peterson a chance to get ahead. Peterson grabbed the Highlander's skirt, attempting to pull him from his horse.

"*Ye damned Sassenach!*"

The second pistol was used well. Sergeant Peterson fell forward, then sideways. His right foot was still in the stirrup, and his body was dragged for fifty feet or more.

But Malcolm had fallen too; the marvel was that he had remained on his horse's back this long. He drew his claymore, rushing at Fitzstephen. The captain laughed and rode past. And Malcolm, frantic, turned to face the muzzles of half a dozen carbines. It would have been suicide to resist. He shrugged his shoulders, and dropped his sword, surrendering with an unexpected mildness.

"It's not the Glenallan you'll be wanting," he told them. "That's an easy thing, taking me. But—let me see you catch the prince!"

They bound him, under the direction of Harris, who was hopelessly out of the chase now. Button had not paused; nor, indeed, had any of the leaders. They were out of sight, and those who made the Highlander prisoner could only tell the direction of the chase by the sound of breaking twigs and the occasional shouts of the captain.

Malcolm sneered.

"There's not a better rider in the world," he declared.

"He'll need wings to get away from Fitzstephen," Harris informed.

"Fitzstephen? Horace Fitzstephen, a captain of the King's Dragoons?"

"That is him, sir."

"So!"

"You have met Captain Fitzstephen?"

Malcolm did not answer. The German's officers, certainly

mere lieutenants, were not for a MacIldowie to converse with. Besides, he had learned enough already.

Meanwhile, to the south, the chase continued. Fitzstephen reflected as he rode that it was very like a hunt. But what a fox! A golden beastie! Fitzstephen believed that he should be able to get at least twenty thousand of the reward, perhaps more. He wondered whether that barbarian had managed to account for Harris with his two-edged sword. He hoped so. Harris was an amiable fellow; but the fewer there were left, the better for the captain.

In any event, there would be the honor of the thing, which in itself could be profitable to a man who knew how to take advantage of it. London would worship him. His credit, for a time, would be without limit . . . He dug the spurs in, straining forward.

The fugitive was not in sight, but Fitzstephen could hear the hoofbeats just ahead.

"Ride, you Roman devil!" he screamed. "Ride like a fiend, but you'll not get away from me!"

For some time they had been going up. They seemed to have no special course. Neither knew the countryside.

They came to a rocky place. On the right and on the left there were precipitous slopes. Ahead was a deep, sharp ravine. Down into this they went, over a brook, up the other side, all without pause.

But now there was a trap. The ground fell away suddenly, in a slope too sharp for descent. Right and left were rocks. There was, on the left, a deep gorge, and on the other side more rocks. The gorge was the only possible avenue of escape. A good horse, if it were fresh, might be able to jump it; but there was no room for a run, and to miss the jump would mean death.

The fugitive tried, unhesitatingly. The animal balked at the edge, wheeled, tried again. But Captain Fitzstephen was out of the ravine by now, and he grabbed the blue coat just as the horse got its courage to spring. The horse failed, and fell to the rocks below with a great crashing of branches and banging of stones. But the rider, hauled off, was saved.

Fitzstephen held a cocked pistol.

"Sir, you are my prisoner!"

The fugitive's hat had fallen off in the tumble, and now there was displayed a great mass of light brown hair. The captain saw also a pair of large blue eyes, a little mouth that exertion had opened, and a tiny chin.

"*By the foul fiend!*"

"It—it was—a good ride—while it lasted, Captain."

He sprang from his horse and grabbed her by the shoulder. "Where's the Pretender? Tell me!"

"The prince?" panted Lady Glenallan, who was seated asprawl at the very edge of the precipice. "Oh, he walked away—while you chased us!"

CHAPTER 19

MALCOLM sat cross-legged on the stone floor, watching Captain Fitzstephen. Fitzstephen stood in the center of this dungeon, and next to him was Lieutenant Harris, a thick-faced, rather timorous officer. A turnkey loitered near the door.

In the past, Malcolm had been a guest in this very castle —a guest of the owner, a cousin, now an exile in France. But Malcolm never before had been in this part of the castle, and had never before been obliged to sit on the pavement.

"For the fortieth time, Jocky, tell me where he is. Careful, now! Think a minute before you answer! The reward is thirty thousand pounds. You never saw that much money, did you? I'll break it in half with you. Fifteen thousand pounds and a passport for you and Lady Helen. I won't say who informed me. Neither will Harris. And I'll answer for the fellow back there."

"Go to the devil."

Fitzstephen frowned. If one prisoner did not tell where the Pretender was concealed, he would have to wring it from the other. And even though Lady Helen Hornsby had married a rank Jacobite, and had presumably been cut off by her father, she still could count many important personages among her friends in London. Fitzstephen did not relish the prospect of becoming harsh with such a lady. Anything he might do to this rebel on the floor would be excused. But Hornsby's daughter was another person.

He tugged at his tunic, scowling.

"You're certain, Jocky? This is the last time I'll ask you to tell us of your own free will."

"Thank the Lord for that!"

"I'm going to use the cat, Jocky—"

Malcolm made no comment. The threat was not a pleasant one to hear, but neither was it unexpected. Indeed, he wondered why it had not come sooner. They had already wasted two hours, and even now they seemed reluctant to wield the whip. Could it be that the butchers were growing weary of blood? Were their stomachs weakening?

Fitzstephen nodded to the turnkey.

This brute, grinning, proudly made known the fact that he had been holding the lash behind him all the while, aware that its use would soon be required. He produced it, rattling the little lead chunks that were fastened on the leather ends.

"Strip him," the captain said coldly.

They pulled off Malcolm's coat and waistcoat and shirt, tying his wrists together again afterward and throwing him face-downward upon the floor. The stones were bitter cold against his cheek.

Fitzstephen took the lash, tickled Malcolm's bare back with it.

"Yell when you're ready to tell me. I'll have it stopped then."

He handed the cat-o'-nine-tails to the turnkey, and that villian began his work. The first blow was no more than a caress, a measure of distance, a swish of little lead chunks over Malcolm's warm skin. The second stung. The third was like a splash of white-hot steel spilled from a crucible.

These came deliberately, well spaced and without hurry. But then the turnkey warmed to his task, and the lash rose and fell with a swiftness and fury that properly befitted the instrument. The thongs whined and hissed in the air, and they smacked with a nasty sound upon the body where long red marks began to appear abruptly and unnaturally, as though they were that many slits of red light thrown through the cracks of a lantern. Blood came out of those marks, very bright and thick. The blood messed over the shoulders, across the neck, and down into the small of the back.

Presently the captain said: "Wait! I think he's fainted. Has he fainted, Lieutenant?"

But before Harris could make an examination, the voice of the laird, remarkably clear and hard, came from under the crossed arms.

"Is it a ten-year-old you think you're dealing with?"

"Hm-m-m . . . Very good, Jocky. A thousand pardons for my stinginess. But I don't want to kill you, unless you oblige me to. Give a cheer for His Majesty King George and we'll let you off for the present."

"Long live King *James!*" Malcolm cried.

Fitzstephen frowned again. Obstinacy like this was annoying. If the Jocky did not submit soon it would be necessary to question Lady Helen. Too great a delay and the Pretender would have been warned.

"We'll go on then. When you're ready to talk, call out. If you can't call, wriggle your fingers."

And the turnkey resumed his work, feet spread wide apart, heels firm on the floor, face still split in a grin that he might have learned under the very tutelage of Lucifer. Again and yet again the lash descended. The thongs became covered with blood; and splashed blood specked out in a small half-circle on the dark stones on either side. But the Glenallan did not move.

There were only those sounds in the room—the whine of the lash, the juicy smacks, and the breathing of the turnkey, which grew heavier and less regular as the beating went on. Fitzstephen and Harris were statue-still, the captain a black cloud of anger, the lieutenant pale and somewhat sick.

Eventually Fitzstephen called another halt. He walked to the prisoner and kicked him twice, hard, in the side.

"Speak up, Jocky. Will you tell us?"

"Is—is he dead?" Harris whispered.

"I doubt it," the captain said coldly, "but he might as well be, for our purposes. If he can stand that much he can stand anything. Let's go upstairs and see his wife."

And they quit the room, the turnkey following them. The turnkey locked the door.

Malcolm had not fainted. There had been moments when he wished that he could, but now he was thankful that God had given him such strength. He had felt the captain's kicks only dully, as though they had been big blunt pushes against his side; for he was, at the moment, almost numbed beyond pain. But in spite of his condition, he had heard every one of the captain's words, and he was frantic with anxiety.

Helen's honor and her fidelity he did not doubt. But the poor girl's spirit had been pounded as though by an enormous, insistent hammer; she was close to panic, he knew, and if they threatened her enough, and bullied her—as they probably would do—they might yet learn where Bonnie Prince Charlie was hidden. For Helen knew. The rendezvous had been arranged before the coming of the dragoons.

He lay still. His back was one burn, as though it had been smeared with oil and then set afire. His head too was hot, and it seemed to be splitting open. His mouth was dry. Down to his very feet he knew the smart of those long red welts as the numbness wore off. The wound in his shoulder, which he had not felt for more than a week, was throbbing heavily, a huge recurring pain.

But it was not this that kept him quiet. For the time, he was weak; but strength was coming back to him. For the time, it would be foolish to struggle with the rope that bound his wrists together. Soon, probably, he would be needing all the strength he possessed: it was a valuable possession, and not to be squandered in the darkness of a dungeon without purpose. So he did not move.

He worried most about Helen. He never ceased to wonder at this wife of his; and there were times when her love was so great that he was actually frightened by it, feeling himself such a wild young fool to be the cause of it. If he could get this business cleared up, if he could see the prince safe in France, and be in France himself, and know that Donald was not in danger—then he could strive with more concentration of effort to be at least partially worthy of Helen Hornsby. God help him, it was not within the power of any man to be more than partially worthy of that lovely thing.

He lay quiet. And an hour, perhaps two hours passed before there was any sound in the corridor outside of the door. Then came the footsteps of the turnkey, who was grinning still when he returned to view his victim at leisure. He peered between the bars of the door. Malcolm did not move.

A key clicked. The fellow was about to inspect this prisoner's clothes. It might be that there was silver in one of the pockets. The turnkey himself would investigate this, since investigation was perfectly safe as long as the prisoner lay in a swoon.

And certainly the prisoner was in a swoon—if he was alive at all. No man, the turnkey believed, would have remained conscious under that lashing.

He entered quietly, leaving the door open against the possible need for a hasty retreat. He'd get the lash himself if he were caught at this. He crossed the room on tiptoe and picked up the rebel's blue coat. It was not a promising garment, for it was faded and dirty, ripped in many places, and patched, frayed at the bottom and at the pocket flaps. But there might be something in it. Meaner pieces of apparel had harbored coins. He began to fumble . . .

Meanwhile, the Laird of Glenallan was getting to his feet. It was a horribly painful process—difficult, too, with his wrists tied before him and his muscles all stiff. His knees and forearms scraped ever so slightly; but the turnkey, engrossed in his search, did not hear these noises. Malcolm, with his tied hands, picked up a stool.

This, too, scraped on the stones, and this the turnkey heard. He whirled around, lifting an arm quickly enough to ward off Malcolm's blow. But the fellow was either too frightened to make a sound or too anxious to get out of this business without being caught by his superiors. And Malcolm, with no such fear and no such anxiety, hit again; and this blow struck. The turnkey fell. Malcolm hit him again on the way down, just to be sure.

Even then Malcolm did not permit himself to hurry. He kept the stool in his hands, and went to the door and listened for the space of at least three minutes. There was a faint sound of footsteps and occasionally a blurred, distant voice, but there was nothing to indicate that this cell or even this corridor would be invaded soon. Satisfied, Malcolm returned to the limp form of the turnkey.

There was a pistol in the belt, but no knife. Malcolm was obliged to free his hands by rubbing the rope against the rough stone of the doorway until it parted. He took the pistol then, examined the priming, and thrust it into his own belt. He donned shirt and waistcoat, in order to cover his back, but he left the ragged coat where it had been when Fitzstephen and the lieutenant quit the room; then he dragged the jailor across the floor and arranged him in a position similar to the one in which he himself had been lying a short while ago.

Then he quit the room, closed and locked the door behind him, and, pistol in hand, started to search for his wife.

CHAPTER 20

BEING A SNOB, Fitzstephen respected Lady Helen for her birth and connections; and being, in this sense at least, a coward, he feared the influence that she might yet summon to her assistance. If he were successful, if he captured the Pretender—then all would be well, for then he would be too great a public hero to be hurt by Lady Helen's friends. But if he failed to get this secret, it might well mean the end of his military career. Poverty and private life combined to make a future he could not view with a smile. And so, partly to give himself courage and partly to have his own attitude formally supported by fellow officers, he conferred with Lieutenant Button and Lieutenant Harris.

"We'll never get it from the Jocky. You saw that, Harris. The man must be made of iron. We must get it from this female if we're to get it at all."

Button suggested: "Perhaps if we twisted her arm—"

"We'd be twisting our epaulettes off, Lieutenant. I tell you I knew this woman in London. I know her relations."

Lady Glenallan was in a large and well-furnished apartment on the second floor of the castle, overlooking, by means of two broad windows, the open court and the high gates that framed the hills beyond. She was seated at one of those windows when the inquisitors entered. She nodded to Fitzstephen, ignoring the others.

Her appearance gave them heart; for her eyes were red from weeping, her face was drawn with worry, and she could not keep her hands motionless in her lap.

Nevertheless, there was a great dignity about her. She had bound up her hair so that it was firmly fixed at the back of her head, with only one truant lock falling over her right shoulder. In the dirty, torn gentleman's coat and waistcoat, and the dirty yellow breeches and stockings, she might well have blushed before these three soldiers: her long fine legs were there for them to view. But she was treating with the enemy, and she was cold. Her pride lent her a classic air.

Fitzstephen bowed, rather annoyed because he was not given a hand to kiss.

"Madam, there is a matter of importance that we must discuss with you. May I beg you to pardon this intrusion and the presence of my fellow officers?"

Lady Helen nodded. She turned her head away from him and stared out of the window. She knew what he was about to demand. She had been thinking of nothing else since her capture.

Fitzstephen watched her closely. He tried to be at once cold and polite; he tried to impress her with his determination and his military authority, at the same time reminding her, by his phrases and fine manners, of the folk she had left in

London, and stimulating with this memory the realization that life was, after all, well worth living.

"Ma'am, I will be frank. You are in no mood for light conversation, and neither am I. But there is something I must know."

"I will never tell you."

So, was Fitzstephen's thought, *she knows!*

He continued, standing right before her and keeping his gaze on her face. He was inexorable.

"This is a matter of life and death, ma'am. Not your life! We are soldiers of His Majesty King George, and we do not molest women. But your husband is our prisoner. He has been a rebel against the Crown, and we are going to hang him."

"You wouldn't dare! Not without a trial!"

"Ma'am, I would hardly dare to do otherwise. I would be reprimanded for going to the trouble and expense of taking such a prisoner back to civilization alive. Your husband is a menace to the peace of the realm. A trial would be folly. He admits his guilt—nay, ma'am, he even boasts it. You yourself admit it."

"I admit that he risked his life for the restoration of his rightful monarch!"

"I shan't enter into a political argument with you now. There is a more important matter to be settled first. Where is the Young Pretender?"

"I will never tell!"

But there was little conviction in the tone. Fitzstephen smiled. The woman had been worn out by the hardships and perils of the wilderness, the furious hide-and-seek she had been playing. She was weak now, frightened.

"Where is he hidden, ma'am?"

She did not answer. She stared out of the window and saw the purple-gray hills, draped in mist, and very far off the glitter of a loch. Her heart beat wildly. She knew that her voice would tremble. She felt as she had felt several times on the long trip from Inverness, when they crossed high places, skirting the edges of cliffs where the rocks swooped down with dizzying straightness. But on those occasions she had always known Malcolm's supporting hand and heard Malcolm's low voice. And now she was alone.

Fitzstephen's position was apparent. He could kill Malcolm and get nothing but praise for the deed. And he would kill Malcolm if stirred to sufficient ire. She sought to delay him, to gain time. But she felt the panic coming . . . And Fitzstephen, obviously, was not prepared to tolerate evasion. Another woman might have pretended to faint; but Lady Helen was no mummer to simulate emotion, nor was the captain a man to be fooled by such a ruse.

"Ma'am, if you'll look a little lower—"

There were three redcoats climbing the high gateway, and one of them carried a rope. A fourth, evidently a corporal, stood underneath directing the work.

"They are to use that as the gallows. Impromptu, but it seemed the most convenient place." He tugged with both hands at the bottom of his waistcoat. He ignored a signal Harris was making, and continued in a quieter voice. "I have promised to be frank with you. Whether here or on the plain, your husband must hang. Surely you realize that. I mean to spare you the agonizing days of suspense and the shame and disgrace of a public execution. You don't know about the executions? I had forgotten that you've been hiding. Let me tell you, then, that the rebels are being hanged and quartered everywhere. There are trials, to be sure, if you wish to call them trials. Do you suppose, ma'am, that your husband would plead not guilty? Do you think that such a plea would have any effect, even if he was to make it?

"Ma'am, the assizes were never so busy and never so

loyal. Jeffries at his drunkest, ma'am, was a seraph com-
pared with these judges." His voice became singsongy. " 'The
judgment of the law is that you, Malcolm Whatever-your-bar-
barian-name-is, return to the prison from whence you came;
from there you must be drawn to the place of execution;
when you come there, you must be hanged by the neck,
but not until you are dead for you must be cut down alive;
then your bowels must be taken out, and burnt before your
face; then your head must be severed from your body, and
your body must be divided into four quarters; and these must
be at the King's disposal. And God Almighty have mercy
on your soul.' You see, I know it by memory, I've heard
it so often recently."

He paused, watching her closely. Her resistance was melt-
ing, and the end was near. He felt it.

"Believe me, this is no child's play, ma'am. You think I can
not hang your husband here and now? That shows how little
you know about the freedom they've given us since Cumberland smashed the clans. That rope you see being strung
will take his life whenever I give a signal from this window.
My word as a soldier for that, ma'am. Do you think I
would boggle at the life of a single rebel? Lord! I thought
you knew me better!"

Lady Helen loved the Stuart and admired him. But there
was no room in her heart for another person when she
thought of Malcolm MacIldowie and the grand strength and
bravery that Malcolm had. A woman must always be decid-
ing. A woman could not be diverse, like a man, and embrace several ideals at once. She was forced to speak for
one and reject all the others.

"If I was to permit your husband to escape, I'd be dis-
graced. But if I was to capture the Pretender, such a petty
blunder would be overlooked and the gratitude of govern-

ment would silence the voices of my enemies. This applies also to my comrades here."

Button spoke up: "I confirm what my captain has said, ma'am. Tell us where the Pretender is and your husband will be permitted to escape. There will be a search, of course, but we can promise that the soldiers will search the wrong places."

Harris contributed: "We can provide passports for the two of you. Before the search is well started, you'll be on your way to France."

Malcolm himself would never tell them. He would hate her for telling. He would fly into a rage when he learned of it. Probably he would throw her off, and certainly he would despise her for the rest of his life. The Laird of Glenallan was no man to be forgiving.

"It could be arranged quietly. No one would know you had gone until a proper period of time had elapsed."

It seemed as though she had plenty of leisure. Hours, it seemed, stretched before her, limitless. She fell to thinking about Bonnie Prince Charlie as she had first seen him when he rode into Edinburgh. She remembered how gay he had been, and how he had waved to the crowds, and remembered, too, how gracefully he sat in saddle.

"I am losing patience, ma'am. The soldiers, I see, have fixed the rope. Unless you give me an answer within five minutes, I shall command that your husband be hanged immediately."

Melodramatic always, he drew a watch; and he faced her, tall, heavy, implacable. Fitzstephen often was a boaster, but she knew that he was telling the truth now. The man was mad for money.

She watched him, dully staring, wondering why she still had that conviction that there was plenty of time; for it seemed to her that there were hours upon hours in which she might meditate.

"Two minutes have passed, ma'am."

She remembered Charlie as she had first seen him in his concealment, after Culloden. Ragged, dirty, filthy even, he had bowed before her, lifting her when she would have curtsied, and kissing her hand as that hand had never been kissed before. He was happy, he had told her, to meet again the wife of the bravest man he had ever known. There was a charm about him that was not earthly . . . There was something of the angel about him, something of the god. Rags and lice, he was yet a prince of the blood royal, a true Stuart, and he had lit the dim hut with a glow of nobility, an expansive, warm, infinitely awesome light that would have quieted a madman and caused a judge to gibber.

"The five minutes have gone, ma'am. Your silence I take as a refusal. Come, Button, Harris. Let's get this dirty business over with."

She remembered the straight hard face of Malcolm—the thin nose, the big strong mouth, the black eyes filled with arrogance. She remembered the way he walked, the way he held his head. And she remembered, too, that old-fashioned thing he called his honor.

She said quietly: "I'll tell you."

The courtly manner dropped from Fitzstephen like an unwanted cloak. His playacting was over. He leaned forward eagerly, the better to catch every syllable. Harris and Button were beside him, and their eyes sparkled like his.

Tears were flowing down Lady Helen's cheeks now—unrestrained—a large and silent torrent. Her heart was breaking.

"He's in a cave at the other end of Glen Allan—on the little hill at your left as you go away from the sea—just underneath two dead pine trees. He—he is alone."

Captain Fitzstephen clapped his hand on his saber hilt.

He grunted for joy, and dashed for the door, disregarding her now that he had learned what he wanted to learn. The men were in the court, saddled and ready. It was a ride of not more than two hours. With Button and with Harris, but a step in advance of both of them, he sprang at the door, swung the door open—

"Damn me!" And he stepped back.

For the barrel of a pistol was pointed at his chest. And behind the pistol was Malcolm MacIldowie Macdomhnull Dhu, the Laird of Glenallan and chief of the clan of that ilk.

He advanced the weapon slightly, stepping forward.

"Go back, Captain. You and I have a quarrel."

CHAPTER 21

THE GLENALLAN was in no hurry. He backed the three officers into the room, nodded rather curtly to his wife, closed the door, and then stood a while considering the situation.

He was not pretty. Wigless, coatless, dirty, sweating, he stood against the wall not only for protection but also to keep from Helen the sight of his back. For he could feel blood oozing through the waistcoat. And Helen, he feared, already had seen too much blood. A great deal might depend upon Helen. He looked at her steadily, impersonally, as though he were seeing her for the first time.

She had risen, but she did not move toward him. She did not know whether he realized what she had told these men. She did not know how long he might have been standing outside the door, nor whether, if he had heard, he would understand the fear that had forced her to speak. But his presence stiffened her, and she stood straight, prepared, now that he was with her, to withstand any storm of threats. Just the knowledge that Malcolm lived filled her with strength. She was still pale, but her shoulders were back, and she had steadied her hands.

Malcolm studied the others, one by one, deliberately and well. From the hall he had not been able to hear what it was Helen told them. But he could guess. The faces of Harris and Button and Fitzstephen betrayed them. Malcolm glanced again at his wife.

"They know?"

She nodded.

Still Malcolm refused to be rushed. This was a delicate place. Ever so slight a move that was a wrong move—and Prince Charlie was dead. These men, then, knew the hiding place. There were three of them, and outside were twenty-odd more, saddled and ready.

In the pistol was Malcolm's advantage. The officers had only their sabers, which none dared to draw. He could kill but one by shooting, but it would be the first one who resisted his commands, and each of them appreciated this.

All three must somehow be prevented from leaving this room, or even shouting out the window. The dragoons were well mounted and all of them were reasonably good horsemen. Even supposing that Malcolm could escape and get a horse, it would not be possible for him to reach the prince before the soldiers did. That one pistol ball at his command was important. He surveyed the situation with care.

Fitzstephen and Button and Harris stood in the center of this big room. They did not try to threaten or to make promises. The Glenallan was no man to be dealt with in that fashion.

Malcolm turned to his wife.

"You are well?"

"Yes."

"Do you feel strong enough to hold a pistol and shoot straight when I tell you to shoot?"

"I could do it for you."

"Be sure!"

"I could do it for you."

He summoned her to where he was standing, and placed her with her back against the heavy door. He handed her the pistol, having cocked it. The three officers he commanded to stand on the opposite side of the room, between the windows.

"Listen to me carefully, Eilidh. You are to shoot through the belly the first of these men who steps away from the place where I put him. But you are not to shoot until I tell you to shoot. Do you understand?"

She was afraid to talk. She braced herself against the door, wetted her lips, and nodded.

The Glenallan, carefully keeping to one side of the room, next addressed himself to the officers.

"Fitzstephen, with you I already have a quarrel. You others, whoever you are, I challenge you to fight to the death because you have invaded my wife's apartment."

He spoke slowly, and never moved his head toward them. He was watching Helen.

"The two that are nearest me draw your swords. The nearest man, hand me his. Keep the point away. I want the hilt."

This was done, and with the utmost care on the part of each man concerned. The pistol, held firmly, still menaced the officers. Lady Helen was a statue.

Saber in hand, the Glenallan turned.

"Now I'll fight you one by one. You first—defend yourself!"

The man he indicated was the one nearest to him, Lieutenant Harris. Now Harris was not a notably fierce man; but a man he was, and he would prefer to go into a duel, even against such an opponent, than be shot like a maimed horse. He advanced to the center of the room. Nervously he saluted, then dropped his blade to guard position. They touched steel—a dry click—and each retreated.

Harris had no wish to attack. Malcolm waited for a full half-minute, studying his enemy's face. It was a half-minute of terrible length for each of the others in the room, Harris included.

Then Malcolm sprang.

It was characteristic of this man that his heart always held his adversaries in contempt, and their ability to fight he by habit belittled. With a claymore, one blow would have finished Harris. But the saber, though easier to swing because of its comparative lightness, was, and for the same reason, easier to parry. Malcolm's first blow was caught and nicely turned, and a riposte caught Malcolm in the left shoulder.

The riposte was light. The lieutenant's sword had scarcely penetrated waistcoat and shirt. But it was unexpected; and if Harris had been a bolder man he might have followed it with another stroke that would have ended the duel. As it was, Malcolm had time to leap back out of measure, his guard high.

He attacked again, this time more warily, with a series of head blows, each one of which was parried, though none was returned.

This Harris was no mean blade. He answered feints only with the tiniest wrist movement, if at all; his parries were never wide; the few cuts he himself made were amazingly quick. But he remained on the defensive, being that kind of man; and Malcolm pressed the attack. The steel rang loudly, the feet scuffled back and forth.

It occurred to Malcolm that the soldiers on the other side of the court might hear these noises. He stepped back, dropping his guard. He listened. Harris stopped gratefully. The castle was quiet. From the yard came only the occasional stamp of a bored horse and the warm distant buzz of conversation. The dragoons might not have heard; or, if they did hear, they might have supposed that their officers were practicing at fence.

Button and Fitzstephen watched the contest from their post between the windows. They did not speak, nor did they move. Neither had much respect for the marksmanship of Lady Helen, but the distance was not great.

Lady Helen watched. Her eyes were popping, and she bit her upper lip.

As for Malcolm, typically he never doubted the outcome. He could feel his own superiority. Yet he was chafed by Harris's defense. Harris was undoubtedly the better fencer. But Malcolm was the better fighter, and why did this thing drag?

Malcolm stepped in again, this time purposely swinging wide. Harris did not even attempt to parry what he mistook for a clumsy shoulder cut. Instead, he lunged. That was precisely what Malcolm had hoped for. Harris's point was easily thrown off, and a strip of bright steel slid between two of Harris's ribs.

Instantly Malcolm turned upon the other two.

"*Stand still!*"

They had not thought to stir. Malcolm pointed to the body of the lieutenant, and spoke to Button.

"Drag that out of the way. Take the saber from it."

Then he spoke to Fitzstephen.

"You're next."

Now Fitzstephen had all the skill that Harris had possessed, and he had heart besides. Moreover, he had been crossed too frequently by this insolent Scot, who now, it would appear, might be taking thirty thousand pounds from under his very nose. Fitzstephen was in a cold rage. His muscles had twitched as he watched Harris defend himself so timorously, and he had marked the times when Harris might

have made cuts if he had been more willing to step closer.
Harris, bluntly, had been frightened.

Fitzstephen gripped his saber, and fell into guard position.
He did not salute.

They touched blades, and Malcolm attacked. The attack
was high. Malcolm had calculated that Fitzstephen, a very
tall man, would be weak in the high line.

Fitzstephen retreated only two steps, slowly. Then he held
ground.

The sabers moved in lively fashion. Neither man hesitated to step into the measure, and neither was afraid of
a counterattack. A down blow, very strong and not soundly
parried, beat Fitzstephen's steel enough to open the skin a-
bove his right ear, and in the same exchange Fitzstephen's
edge grazed the Glenallan's right temple, letting a little
blood.

Either of these two touches, almost simultaneous, would
have been excuse enough to stop an ordinary affair of
honor. But this was not an ordinary affair of honor. There
were no seconds, there was no referee, no cartel, and it was
granted by both men that there would be no quarter.

Nor was there an instant's letup. It did not seem possible
that the two could engage so closely and remain alive. The
blades were both busy; they swished the air, glittering,
ringing, sometimes sending out sparks when they struck . . .

Lieutenant Button, open-mouthed, watched the best sword-
play it had ever been his fortune to witness. Lady Helen
still did not stir; but now her hand trembled, the hand
that held the gun. She had caught a glimpse of Malcolm's
back, and this, together with the sight of the blood on Malcolm's face, had so scared her that she did not know how
much longer she could stand.

In a corner near one of the windows was the corpse that

had been Harris. It was grotesquely hunched over, as though he had been shot in the guts while seated.

"This for Martin's, Jocky!"

Malcolm parried, and made a savage return for the right flank.

"This for Dafty!"

Malcolm tried a low guard, holding his blade in prime position and cutting repeatedly for the body. Fitzstephen refused to try for the head then, but held his hand low with his point directed at Malcolm's eyes.

Fitzstephen's thrust and cuts were shorter but a trifle quicker than Malcolm's. Fitzstephen kept his blade in line better, being accustomed to fencing with the small sword, while Malcolm was used to the heavy claymore. Malcolm moved quickly in and out. Fitzstephen wasted no steps, but he was quite as quick when he did move.

They were perfectly matched. But the Lady of Glenallan did not know this. Already near collapse, she had been so terrorized by the fight that she was not able to hold her knees stiff or to keep hand and arm steady. It happened that the English captain was, at this moment, pressing the attack—advancing regularly, step by tiny careful step, forcing Malcolm to back away. This attack was delivered with extraordinary speed and force; but it did not trouble Malcolm, who retreated with care, watching for a false move.

Lady Helen did not realize this. To her it seemed that Malcolm was about to be killed. She could no longer control her battered nerves. She closed her eyes, put her right arm out at full length, tightened her grip on the pistol . . .

The explosion paralyzed the three men, who had forgotten all about the pistol.

Button, who had been leaning forward, straightened with a jerk. Fitzstephen and the Glenallan gaped at one another through the moving smoke, instinctively stepping back out of the measure.

Helen's arm fell to her side. The pistol clattered on the floor, and Lady Helen slipped to her knees, half fainting.

The ball had done no more than knock some chips from the wall between the windows.

Button jumped first. He reached the door, pushed Lady Helen aside. But in doing this he turned his back on Lady Helen's husband, who promptly cut open the lieutenant's head with a heavy down blow.

Fitzstephen, encircling both men, got through the door and slammed it behind him. Malcolm reached the hallway only in time to see him disappear around a turn, yelling.

Malcolm went back into the room, closed the door behind him, put a table against it. A glance showed him that Button was dead. That man lay perfectly still, pitched forward on his face, within a few inches of Lady Helen.

Helen herself was on hands and knees, trying to get up. Malcolm lifted her in his arms, deposited her in a chair, and went to one of the windows.

He saw the dragoons scamper toward their horses, while other dragoons came swarming from the two doors on the right of the court. Then he saw Fitzstephen, hatless but still holding his saber, and still yelling.

"Mount, you fools! After me—every man of you!"

Malcolm saw the whole troop mount with a smoothness and precision that made him, even at that moment, envy them their horsemanship. He saw them wheel, fall into place, and gallop out under the gate, beautifully spaced, their captain at their head, their plumes tossing, each with his carbine cradled in his right arm.

He turned back to Helen, and shook her vigorously.

"Can you run?"

She blinked, a rag in his arms. But there was vast relief in her eyes.

"Malcolm, I couldn't help it. I thought he was about to kill you."

"Can you run?"

"If you're with me."

He yanked her to her feet, shoved her into the hall. There was one chance left. If Helen could keep up with him, if he could remember a path without a single misstep, and if the men were still at the cave . . .

CHAPTER 22

THEY HAD placed Helen behind a large rock, and Malcolm instructed her not to stir.

"One of Patrick's men will take care of you if I get killed," he had told her. "You shouldn't be here at all, but I'll not be letting you get far away from me again."

Now he was superintending the distribution of the muskets. Peeping from behind her rock, she watched him. They had run or walked very fast the whole distance, and Malcolm had carried her for more than a mile, yet though she was still breathing hard he seemed unruffled.

"It's a grand lot of guns, Patrick. You took them from the Saxons?"

"Aye."

There were eight men and fifteen muskets. In addition, Patrick Grant had equipped Malcolm with a pistol and a claymore; and only two of the robbers lacked swords.

Malcolm bit off the end of a waxed-paper cartridge and poured gunpowder into the barrel of a Brown Bess that once had been shouldered by one of King George's men; he dropped the ball on top of the powder, crumpled the waxed paper and stuffed this in for wadding, and then jammed down with the ramrod. They were all loading muskets and stacking them against trees to await his orders. It might start to rain at any moment, and there would be no time to reload anyway, even if the powder was dry.

"Eight of them here, each man wherever he can hide best. Then the rest of them down by those rocks."

Patrick Grant was respectful, but dubious.

"Are you sure they must come this way, Macdomhnull Dhu?"

"Aye."

"But—"

Malcolm fairly snarled at him.

"Do I no' ken my own country, dolt!"

Patrick Grant was silent after that.

The weapons placed, there was nothing to do but wait. It had started to rain, a drizzle. The Seven Men of Glenmoriston, by no means unaccustomed to attacking several times their number, were not nervous: they hid themselves quickly, adroitly, seemed to melt into the landscape. Malcolm walked up to where Helen sat.

"Don't you fear they might have come and gone already?"

He shook his head.

"The ground's too soft for them to go fast."

He was worried, but not about that. His one fear now was that Prince Charlie, who had carried a pistol, might have killed himself rather than submit to capture, or might have been killed when he threatened to fight. It was a terrible thought, that Prince Charles might be dead.

"Are—are you just going to stay here and shoot down?"

"No. They'd gallop off with him."

"But you can't charge a whole company of them!"

He had been staring up the glen, up past ruined Allan's Castle. Maybe he was thinking of Fergus. Helen thought she had never seen him look so dark, black-browed, dangerous.

"We can, lassie, and we will. But you must stay here. I don't want you to even peep out. It—won't be bonnie."

He leaned over, and lifted her chin, and kissed her.

"My brave Eilidh. My brave, brave wife," he murmured.

But he straightened, glanced up the glen again, glanced down the slope where the Seven Men of Glenmoriston were concealed.

"Remember, don't move," he whispered; and he went away.

She did move. Waiting motionless was too great a strain. After a long time—it seemed an hour but it might have been but a few minutes—she peered around the edge of the rock. The glen was as she had first seen it—utterly desolate. The dark broken castle was a dead thing at the edge of a dead lake. Nothing stirred, and there was no sound. The clouds, black and harsh, scuttled past so low that they scraped the hilltops and seemed to be trying to reach down into the glen and claim it for their own.

Helen looked down the slope. There was no sign of any human being, though she knew that somewhere among the bracken and the rock eight men lay staring with steel-hard eyes along eight musket barrels. She could not see a bonnet, a feather, a glint of metal. She thought that if no word were spoken soon, if no sound were made, she would go mad. She sat back on the ground abruptly, ducking her head, biting her lips, to control jumpy nerves.

When next she looked up the glen she saw something that moved. The rain was a thin, dreary drizzle, and the clouds were very low and dark; but even through the murk and mist she could see something moving.

She watched, fascinated, straining her eyes. It was the dragoons. At first she knew them rather by their motion

than by any detail her eyes could pick up. Then she began
to see them more clearly, as individuals.

The utter silence continued. Had Malcolm and the Seven
Men seen the dragoons? Should she shout down to them?
She decided not to.

The cavalcade moved gingerly over wet and treacherous
ground. It would be obliged to go past the very bottom of
the slope, so narrow was the glen at this point. It was a
perfect place for an ambush, as no doubt the boy Malcolm
MacIldowie had many times reflected. The horsemen would
be caught in a spot where they'd be crowded together, unable
to see the enemy who was shooting down on them, unable
to maneuver unless they first dismounted. The breeze was
blowing down that slope toward the narrow pass: it would
carry the smoke of the first volley into the eyes of the
soldiers and would cover the shifting of the hidden men to
their second line of muskets.

She waited. She watched the unsuspecting men come
closer and closer. But nothing happened, and there was no
sound. They were so close now that she could hear the
creak of their saddlestraps, the wet slog of hoofs.

Prince Charles was in their midst, his wrists tied behind
his back. Beside him, proudly smiling, was Captain Fitzstephen. Perhaps the captain was the happier because his
two lieutenants were no longer alive to share that reward
with him; he would have it all to himself, except for some
trifling sums thrown to the soldiers.

The dragoons were passing along the very bottom of the
slope now, breaking into double file and walking their horses
carefully over the marshy, hummocky ground. Prince Charles,
his chin on his chest, was jogged back and forth; he was like
a corpse, limp and lifeless, crushed by humiliation. Only a
horseman's instinct kept him in saddle.

Lady Helen almost rose in her place. Were they going

to let these scoundrels pass? Had they become afraid, crouching in the bracken there? Why didn't they fire? Why didn't they fight?

Then there came an explosion that smashed the whole vast silence of the glen, shaking the very rocks, seeming to scare back the very clouds. The eight muskets had crashed as one. The echoes banged back and forth, up and down Glen Allan. Ripping through this hollow roar were shrieks, war cries.

Then on the slope there was silence again. Helen knew that the attackers had moved lower down under the cover of their own gunsmoke. As that smoke rolled across the pass she saw a wild group of soldiers, some of them on the ground, some tugging at the reins of their stamping, rearing mounts. The dragoons' horses were for transportation, not battle. Unlike regular cavalry mounts, they had not been trained to coolness under gunfire.

Fitzstephen, she saw in that glance, was pushing Prince Charles back up the glen; and Charles himself had raised his head and was staring with wild hope at the hillside, blinking in the sharp smoke.

Some English soldiers raised their carbines, and Helen ducked back of the rock again. She heard another perfectly timed volley, more war cries.

Presently Patrick Grant was standing beside her. He was out of breath and perspiring, but impassive as an Oriental.

"MacDomhnull Dhu says Prince Charlie is safe."

"It—it's all over, already?"

"Aye."

"But what is Sir Malcolm doing? Is he safe?"

"Aye, he's safe. He wants to fight the big *siler roy* but Charlie will no' allow it."

She stood up. At the bottom of the slope, where a few minutes ago the cavalcade had been filing past, was a frightened, cowed, unarmed group of soldiers, all dismounted. Some of the horses were stretched out on the ground, still kicking. Some of the soldiers, too, were lying down. They might have been dead. Anyway, the Glenmoriston men were going through their pockets, systematically and without hurry.

Prince Charles she marked instantly. By his rags alone he might have been a member of Patrick Grant's robber band, but he had still that air of high dignity. Malcolm was before him, holding a bare cavalry saber under each arm and obviously pleading. Nearby stood the glowering Fitzstephen.

She ran down the slope, stumbling, calling. Fitzstephen raised his eyebrows when she appeared, and he even made a little bow. Some of the soldiers gasped stupidly, as though at a vision. Prince Charles bowed low.

"I am delighted to see you safe, Lady Glenallan. If you had been hurt in helping us I should have been inconsolable."

He kissed her hand.

"Your Highness, don't let them fight any more!"

"I have forbidden it. Will a MacIldowie disobey me?"

Malcolm did not move. Helen had never seen his face so dark. Dark naturally, made darker by sun and rain, now rage was pounding the blood there so that it was almost black. He glared at the ground.

"If Your Royal Princeship will deign to change his royal mind," Fitzstephen put in sarcastically, "I might as well be killed after I've sliced this upstart. We have a private quarrel. And these savages will tear me to pieces anyway, the minute your back is turned. The Glenmoriston gang is not noted for its clemency to prisoners."

"I have forbidden it," Charles Edward said again. "There must be no settling of private quarrels while the war is on."

"The war, as you call it, is over," Fitzstephen pointed out.

Charles Edward Stuart responded promptly.

"This war, sir, is never over. It will never be over until the right side has prevailed. We are not defeated. We are only suspending our struggle."

Fitzstephen deliberately turned away from him. He faced Malcolm, who did not look up.

"If *you* can't disobey this false prince, Jocky, *I* can!"

He jerked one of the sabers from under Malcolm's arm. "Defend yourself, sir!"

Helen screamed. Charles Edward stepped forward, crying something that nobody heard.

But it was ended very quickly. Malcolm sprang back, parrying once. Fitzstephen, snorting like a bull, plunged after him. Fitzstephen was overexcited perhaps, too eager. Malcolm caught the stroke high on his own blade and cut back with a complete overhand motion. It was the kind of riposte only a very courageous man in certain circumstances, or a fool, would attempt. It caught Fitzstephen exactly on top of his head, and the big captain of dragoons pitched forward on his face. There was no need to examine him. The whole top of his skull was crushed.

On an ordinary day you could not have found a spot in the world more deserted and few spots more difficult of access, whether by land or by sea, than the fjord of Lochnanaugh. You might have supposed, standing at the base of the rocks, that Time had reversed her spool and left you in the middle of a primeval forest untainted by the foot of man.

Lochnanaugh had known briefly the *Doutelle*, that jaunty little sea adventurer in which Bonnie Prince Charles had come to raise rebellion and strife in the land. The *Doutelle* had sailed back to France, Charles had marched inland, and the bay had returned to its slumbers, convinced that it would never be disturbed again.

But now another French vessel was in the offing, and once

more the serenity of Lochnanaugh was shocked by man-made excitement. The ship itself was crowded: along its rails were outcasts who were taking their last look at the land of their birth. And along the shore were Highlanders in blue bonnets, taking their last look at the prince and their friends and cousins.

Charles Edward kept his right arm stiff and high in salute to those on the shore. His bonnet was in his right hand. Always he had a sense of the dramatic; and he knew that the tale of how he had sailed away would be told and retold at countless firesides.

"I will come back!" he cried, and his voice rang clear across the water. "*I will come back!*"

The rest of the gentlemen said nothing. They only stared at Scotland.

Rain clouds were hurrying up behind them. Though it was midday, soon the scene would be dark and wet. But for the moment it was all bright sunshine, a calm serene clear day. You could see the upthrust of beautiful Ben Alder, to which the landscape led with waves of heavy green pine trees. You could almost see Ben Nevis. For that moment the western Highlands were basking in a strange and awesome peace.

Then the storm broke, and abruptly the Highlands were sullen again, brooding, dreaming their ancient melancholy dream.

Charles Edward Stuart relaxed his pose; they were too far from shore now to make it effective. He dropped his hand on the nearest shoulder, the left shoulder of the last Mac-Ildowie. And the two men stood there gazing through rain at the outlines of the mist-blurred shore.

"It's a braw country, Glenallan," said Charles Edward Stuart.

"Aye," said Malcolm.